"It's crazy, isn't it? I shouldn't feel anything for you. But you… I mean, look, I know it's chemistry, or whatever, I know it's not feelings. But…"

She bit her full lower lip and looked up at him from beneath her lashes, the expression both innocent and coquettish. "Don't you think that maybe we should have a chance to taste it before I'm sold into marriage?"

She planted her hand on his chest. And Javier knew that she could feel it then. Feel his heart raging against the muscle and blood and bone there. Feel it raging against everything that was good and right and real.

She let out a shaking breath, and he could feel the heat of it brush his mouth, so close was she. So close was his destruction.

He was iron. He was rock. He had been forced to become so. A man of nothing more than allegiance to an ideal. Knowing with absolute certainty that if he should ever turn away from that, he might become lost. That corruption might take hold of him in the way that it had done his father. Because he considered himself immune to nothing.

And so, he had made himself immune to everything.

Except for this. Except for her.

Millie Adams has always loved books. She considers herself a mix of Anne Shirley (loquacious but charming and willing to break a slate over a boy's head if need be) and Charlotte Doyle (a lady at heart, but with the spirit to become a mutineer should the occasion arise). Millie lives in a small house on the edge of the woods, which she finds allows her to escape in the way she loves best—in the pages of a book. She loves intense alpha heroes and the women who dare to go toe-to-toe with them (or break a slate over their heads).

Books by Millie Adams

Harlequin Presents

The Kings of California
The Scandal Behind the Italian's Wedding

Visit the Author Profile page at Harlequin.com.

Millie Adams

—

STEALING THE PROMISED PRINCESS

HARLEQUIN
PRESENTS

H HARLEQUIN®
PRESENTS®

Recycling programs
for this product may
not exist in your area.

ISBN-13: 978-1-335-89409-0

Stealing the Promised Princess

Copyright © 2020 by Millie Adams

This edition published by arrangement with Harlequin Books S.A.

For questions and comments about the quality of this book,
please contact us at CustomerService@Harlequin.com.

Harlequin Enterprises ULC
22 Adelaide St. West, 40th Floor
Toronto, Ontario M5H 4E3, Canada
www.Harlequin.com

Printed in U.S.A.

STEALING THE PROMISED PRINCESS

For all the Harlequin Presents novels that came before this one. It is the other books, and the other authors, that brought me my love of romance. And it is why I'm writing them now.

CHAPTER ONE

"I HAVE A debt to collect, Violet King."

Violet stared out the windows of her office, glass all around, providing a wonderful view of the Pacific Ocean directly across her desk, with a view of her staff behind her. There were no private walls in her office space. She preferred for the team to work collaboratively. Creatively.

Her forward-thinking approach to business, makeup and fashion was part of why she had become one of the youngest self-made billionaires in the world.

Though, self-made might be a bit of a stretch considering that her father, Robert King, had given her the initial injection of cash that she needed to get her business off the ground. Everyone worked with investors, she supposed. That hers was genetically related to her was not unheard-of nor, she supposed, did it fully exclude her from that self-made title. But she was conscious of it. Still, she had made that money back and then some.

And she did *not* have debt.

Which meant this man had nothing to say to her.

"You must have the wrong number," she said.

"No. I don't."

The voice on the other end of the phone was rich and dark, faintly accented, though she couldn't quite nail down what accent it was. Different to her family friend, now her sister's husband, Dante, who was from Italy and had spent many years in the States since then. Spanish, perhaps, but with a hint of Brit that seemed to elongate his vowels.

"Very confident," she said. "But I am in debt to no man."

"Oh, perhaps I misspoke then. You are not in debt. You are the payment."

Ice settled in her stomach. "How did you get this number?"

In this social media age where she was seemingly accessible at all hours, she guarded her private line with all the ferocity of a small mammal guarding its burrow. She—or her assistants—might be available twenty-four hours a day on the internet, but she could only be reached at this line by business associates, family or personal friends. This man was none of those, and yet somehow he was calling her. And saying the most outlandish things.

"How I got this number is not important to the conversation."

She huffed. "To the contrary, it is extremely important."

Suddenly, she felt the hairs on the back of her neck stand on end and she turned around. The office building was empty, just as she thought it was. It was late in the day and everyone had gone home. Her employees often worked from home, or at the beach, wherever creativity struck them.

Her team wanted to be there, and she didn't need to enforce long office hours for them to do their work. The glass walls of the building made it possible for her to see who was in residence at all times, again, not so she could check up on them, but so there was a sense of collaboration.

It also made it easy to see now that she was alone here.

Of course she was. A person couldn't simply walk into this building. Security was tight, and anyone wanting entrance would have to be buzzed in.

But then suddenly she saw a ripple of movement through the outermost layer of glass, motion as a door opened. A dark shape moved through each clear barrier, from room to room, like a shark gliding beneath the surface of clear water. As each door opened, the shape moved closer, revealing itself to be the figure of a man.

Her chest began to get tight. Fear gripped her, her heart beating faster, her palms damp.

"Are you here?" she whispered.

But the line went dead, and she was left standing frozen in her office, her eyes glued to the man steadily making his way deeper and deeper into the office building. The glass, however transparent, was bulletproof, so there was that.

There were so many weirdos in the world that an abundance of caution never went amiss. She had learned about that at a fairly early age. Her father being one of the wealthiest businessmen in California had put her in the public eye very young. The media had always been fascinated with their family; with her brother, who was incredibly successful in his own right; her mother, who was a great beauty. And then, with her for the same reason.

It had always felt so…unearned to her. This great and intense attention for doing nothing at all. It had never sat well with her.

Her father had told her to simply enjoy it.

That she was under no obligation to do anything, considering he'd done all the work already.

He'd always been bemused by her desire to get into business, but he'd helped her get started. He'd been humoring her, that much had been clear. But she'd been determined to prove to him that she was smart. That she could make it on her own.

Even now she had the feeling he regarded her billion-dollar empire as a hobby.

The only one of them who had seemingly escaped without massive amounts of attention was her younger sister, Minerva, who Violet had always thought might have been the smartest of them all. Minerva had made herself into the shape of something unremarkable so that she could live life on her own terms.

Violet had taken a different approach, and there were times when the lack of privacy grated and she regretted living the life that she had.

Sometimes she felt an ache for what might have been. She wondered why she had this life. Why she was blessed with money and a certain amount of success instead of being anonymous or impoverished.

Some of that was eased by the charity she ran with her sister, which made it feel like all of it did mean something. That she had been granted this for a reason. And it made the invasions of privacy bearable.

Though not so much now. She felt vulnerable, and far too visible, trapped in a glass bowl of her own making, only able to watch as a predator approached her, and she was unable to do anything but wait.

She tried to call the police, her fingers fumbling on the old-fashioned landline buttons. It wasn't working. She had that landline for security. For privacy. And it was failing her on every level.

Of course she had her cell phone, but it was…

Sitting on the table just outside the office door.

And then suddenly he was *there*. Standing right on the other side of her office door. Tall, broad, clad all in black, wearing a suit that molded to his exquisitely hard-looking body, following every cut line from the breadth of his shoulders to his tapered waist, on down his long muscular legs. He turned around, and how he saw she was thinking of him in those terms she didn't know. Only that he was a force. Like looking at a sheer rock face with no footholds.

Hard and imposing, looming before her.

His face was…

Like a fallen Angel. Beautiful, and a sharp, strange contrast to the rest of him.

There was one imperfection on that face. A slashed scar that ran from the top of his high cheekbone down to the corner of his mouth. A warning.

This man was dangerous.

Lethal.

"Shall we have a chat?"

The barrier of the glass between them made that deep, rich voice echo across the surface of it, and she could feel it reverberating inside of her.

She hated it.

"How did you get in here?"

"My darling, I have a key."

She shrank back. "I'm not your darling."

"True," he said. "You are not. But you are my quarry. And I have found you."

"I'm not very hard to find," she said. She lifted her chin, trying to appear confident. "I'm one of the most famous women in the world."

"So you are. And that has me questioning my brother's sanity. But I am not here to do anything but follow orders."

"If you're here to follow orders, then perhaps you should follow one of mine. Leave."

"I answer to only one man. To only one person. And it is not you."

"A true regret," she said tightly.

"Not for me."

"What do you want?"

"I told you. I am here to collect payment. And that payment is you."

She was beautiful. But he had been prepared for that. When his brother had told him that it was finally time for him to make good on a promise given to him by Robert King ten years ago, Prince Javier de la Cruz had held back a litany of questions for his lord and master. He wondered why his brother wished to collect the debt now. And why he wished to collect it at all, at least in the form of this woman.

She was conspicuous. And she was everything his brother was not. Modern. Painfully so in contrast with the near medieval landscape of Monte Blanco. Yes, the kingdom had come a long way under his brother's rule during the last two years, but there was still a long way to go to bring it out of the Dark Ages their father had preferred. If a woman such as Violet King would be something so foreign to their people, then imagining her his queen was impossible.

But then, on some level, Javier imagined that was his brother's aim. Still, it was not Javier's position to question. Javier was as he had ever been. The greatest weapon Monte Blanco possessed. For years, he had undermined his father, kept the nation from going to war, kept his people safe. Had freed prisoners when they were wrongfully withheld. Had done all that he could to ensure that his father's impact on their people was as minimal as possible. And he had done so all under the oversight of his older brother, who—when he had taken control—had immediately begun to revive the country, using the money that he had earned with his business acumen. The Tycoon King, he was called.

And this—this deal with Robert King—had been one of those bargains he'd struck in secret. Apparently this deal had been made long ago, over drinks in a casino in Monte Carlo. A bet the other man had lost.

Javier was surprised his brother would hold a man to a drunken bargain.

And yet, here he was.

But Matteo was not a thoroughly modern man, whatever moves he was making to reform the country, and this sort of medieval bargain was just the type he knew his brother might favor.

Still…

Looking at her now, Javier could not imagine it.

She was wearing a white suit. A crisp jacket and loose-fitting pants. Her makeup was like a mask in his estimation. Eyelashes that seemed impossibly long, full lips played up by the gloss that she wore on her mouth. A severe sort of contour created in her cheeks by whatever color she had brushed onto them.

Her dark hair was in a low ponytail, sleek and held back away from her face.

She was stunningly beautiful. And very young. The direct opposite of their poor mother, who had been so pale and defeated by the end of her life. And perhaps that was the point.

Still, forcing a woman into marriage was possibly not the best way to go about proving your modernity.

But again. He was not in a position to argue.

What mattered most was his brother's vision for the country, and he would see it done.

He was a blunt instrument. Not a strategist.

Something he was comfortable with. There was an honesty to it. His brother had to feign diplomacy. Had to hide his agenda to make the world comfortable.

Javier had to do no such thing.

"I don't know who you are. And I don't know what you're talking about," she said.

He made his way over to the door, entered in the code and it unlocked.

Her father had given him all that information. Because he knew that there was no other choice.

She backed against her desk, her eyes wide with fear.

"What are you doing?"

"This is growing tiresome. I'm Prince Javier de la Cruz, of Monte Blanco. And you, Violet King, are my brother's chosen bride."

"What?" She did something he did not expect at all. She guffawed. It was the most unladylike sound he had ever heard. "I am *nobody's* chosen bride."

"You are. Your father owes my brother a debt. Apparently, he ran out of capital at a gambling table and was quite…in his cups, so to speak. He offered you. And I have come to collect you."

"My father would not do such a thing. He would not…gamble me away. My brother, on the other hand, might play a prank on me that was this ridiculous. Are there cameras somewhere? Am I on camera?"

"You are not on camera," he said.

She laughed again. "I must be. If this is your attempt to get a viral video or something, you better try again. My father is one of the most modern men that I have ever known. He would never, ever sell one of his daughters into marriage. You know my sister came home from studying abroad with a baby, and he didn't even ask where the baby came from. He just kind of let her bring it into his house. He does not treat his daughters like commodities, and he does not act like he can sell us to the highest bidder."

"Well, then perhaps you need to speak to him."

"I don't need to speak to him, because this is ridiculous."

"If you say so."

And so he closed the distance between them, lifted her up off the ground and threw her over his shoulder. He was running low on time and patience, and he didn't have time to stand around being laughed at by some silly girl. That earned him a yelp and a sharp kick to his chest. Followed by another one, and then another.

Pain was only pain. It did not bother him.

He ignored her.

He ignored her until he had successfully transported her out of the building, which was conveniently empty, and down to the parking lot where his limo was waiting. Only then, when he had her inside with the doors closed and locked, did she actually stare at him with fear. Did she actually look like she might believe him?

"Violet King, I am taking you back to my country. Where you are to be Queen."

CHAPTER TWO

SHE DIDN'T HAVE her phone. She might as well have had her right hand amputated. She had no way to reach anybody. She was an undisputed queen of social media. And here she was, sentenced to silence, told she was going to be Queen of a nation, which was something else entirely.

But this guy was clearly sick in the head, so whatever was happening…

She looked around the limousine. He might be sick in the head, but he also had someone bankrolling his crazy fantasy.

"Is this your limousine?"

He looked around and rolled his shoulders back, settling into the soft leather. "No."

"Who are you working for?"

"I told you. My brother. The King of Monte Blanco."

"I don't even know where that is."

She searched her brain, trying to think if she

had ever heard of the place. Geography wasn't her strong suit, but she was fairly well traveled, considering her job required it. Also, she loved it. Loved seeing new places and meeting new people. But Monte Blanco was not on her radar.

"It's not exactly a hot tourist destination," he said.

"Well."

"It's not my brother's limousine either, if you are curious. Neither of us would own something so..." His lip curled. "Ostentatious."

Old money. She was familiar enough with old money and the disdain that came with it. She was new money. And often, the disdain spilled over onto her. She was flashy. And she was obvious. But her fortune was made by selling beauty. By selling flash. Asking women to draw attention to themselves, telling them that it was all right. To dress for themselves. To put makeup on to please themselves, not necessarily to please men.

So yes, of course Violet herself was flashy. And if he had an issue with it, he could go... Well, jump out of the limo and onto the busy San Diego Freeway. She would not mourn him.

"Right. So you're a snob. A snob who's somehow involved in a kidnapping plot?" She supposed, again, he could be an actor.

Not someone wealthy at all. Somebody hired to play a prank on her.

Somebody hired to hurt her.

That thought sent a sliver of dread through her body. She wouldn't show it. After all, what good were layers of makeup if you couldn't use them to hide your true face?

"I'm not a snob. I'm a prince."

"Right. Of a country I've never heard of."

"Your American centric viewpoint is hardly my problem, is it, Ms. King? It seems to me that your lack of education does not speak to my authenticity."

"Yes. Well. That is something you would say." The car was still moving, farther and farther away from where they had originated. And she supposed that she had to face the fact that this might not be a joke. That this man really thought she was going to go back to his country with him. If that country existed. Really, she had nothing but his word for it, and considering that he seemed to think that she was going to marry his brother, he might be delusional on multiple levels.

"I want to call my dad."

"You're welcome to," he said, handing her the phone.

She snatched it from him and dialed her father's personal number as quickly as possible. Robert King picked up on the second ring.

"Dad," she said, launching into her proclamation without preamble. "A madman has bundled me up and put me in his limousine, and he's claiming that you made a deal with him some decade ago, and I'm supposed to marry his brother?"

"I didn't make a deal with your dad," Javier said. "My brother did."

"It doesn't matter," she hissed. And then she sat there, waiting for her father to respond. With shock, she assumed. Yes, she assumed that he would respond with shock. Because of course this was insane. And of course it was the first time her father was hearing such a thing. Because there was no way he had anything to do with this. "So anyway, if you could just tell him that he's crazy…"

She realized how stupid it was the minute she said that. Because of course her father telling Javier he was crazy wouldn't likely reinforce it if the act of flinging her into his limousine hadn't done it.

"Violet…" Her father's voice was suddenly rough, completely uncharacteristic of the smooth, confident man that she had always looked up to.

Her father was imperfect. She wasn't blind

to that. The fact that he was completely un-invested in her success was obvious to her. When it came to her brother, he was always happy to talk business. But because her business centered around female things, and she herself was a woman, she could never escape the feeling that her father thought it was some kind of hobby. Something insubstantial and less somehow.

But surely he wouldn't... Surely that didn't mean he saw her as currency.

"He's crazy, right?"

"I never thought that he would follow up on this," her father said. "And when you reached your twenties and he didn't... I assumed that there would be no recourse."

"You promised me to a king?"

"It could've been worse. I could have promised you to the used car salesman."

"You can't just promise *someone else* to *someone else*. I'm a person, not a... A cow."

"I'm sorry," he said. "Violet, I honestly didn't think that..."

"I won't stand for it. I will not do it. What's to stop me from jumping out of the car right now—" she looked out the window and saw the scenery flying by at an alarming clip, and she knew that that would keep her from jumping out of the car, but her father didn't need to know that "—and running for freedom?"

"The businesses. They will go to him."

"The businesses?"

"Yours and mine. Remember we sheltered yours under mine for taxes and…"

"Maximus's too?"

Because if he had sheltered her business, surely he had sheltered her brothers as well…

"No," her father said slowly.

"What's the real reason you kept mine underneath your corporation? Was it for this?"

"No. Just that I worried about you. And I thought that perhaps…"

"Because you don't think anything of me. You don't think that I'm equal to Maximus. If you did, then you wouldn't have done this to me. I can't believe… I can't believe you."

She could keep on arguing with her father, or she could accept the fact that he had sold her as chattel to a stranger. And with that realization, she knew that she needed to simply get off the phone. There was no redeeming this. Nothing at all that would fix it.

She had come face-to-face with how little she meant to her father, how little he thought of her.

She had taken his reaction to Minerva coming home with the baby to mean that he was enlightened, but that wasn't it at all. Minerva was being traditional, even if she hadn't had a husband initially when she had brought the baby home.

Still, he would rather have seen Minerva, in all her quirky glory, with a baby, than see Violet as a serious businesswoman.

There was no talking to him. She stared across the limo at the man who had taken her captive, and she realized...

That he was a saner option than arguing with her father.

She hung up the phone.

"So you are telling the truth."

"I have no investment in lying to you," Javier said. "I also have no investment in this deal as a whole. My brother has asked that I retrieve you, and so I have done it."

"So, you're a Saint Bernard, then?"

A flash of icy amusement shot through his dark eyes, the corner of his mouth curving up in a humorless smile. "You will find that I am not so easily brought to heel, I think."

"And yet here you are," she said. "Doing the bidding of someone else."

"Of my king. For my country. My brother and I have been the stronghold standing between Monte Blanco and total destruction for over a decade. My father was always a dictator, but his behavior spiraled out of control toward the end of his life. We were the only thing that kept his iron fist from crushing our people. And now we seek to rebuild. Who my brother wants as his choice of bride is his business. And if you'll excuse me… I don't care one bit for your American sensibilities. For your money. For your achievements. I care only that he has asked for you, and so I will bring you to him."

"Good boy," she said.

His movements were like liquid fury. One minute he was sitting across from her in the limousine, and the other he was beside her. He gripped her chin and held her fast, forcing her to look into his eyes. But there was no anger there. It was black, and it was cold. And it was the absence of all feeling that truly terrified her.

She did not think he would hurt her.

There was too much control in his hold. He was not causing her any pain. She could feel the leashed strength at the point where his thumb and forefinger met her chin.

"I am loyal," he said. "But I am not good. The cost of keeping my country going, the cost of my subterfuge has been great. Do not ever make the mistake of thinking that I'm good."

And then he withdrew from her. It was like

she had imagined it. Except she shivered with the cold from those eyes, so she knew she hadn't.

"How are you going to make me get on the plane?"

"I will carry you," he said. "Or you could get on with your own two feet. Your father won't harbor you. I assume that he told you as much. So there's no use you running back home, is there?"

She was faced then with a very difficult decision. Because he was right—she could try to run away. But he would overpower her. And she had a feeling that no one would pay much attention to what would look like a screaming match between two rich people, culminating with her being carried onto a private plane. They were far too adjacent to Hollywood for anybody to consider that out of the ordinary.

And even if she did escape... Her father had verified what he'd said. Her father saw nothing wrong with using her to get out of a bad situation. He had sacrificed not only her, but her livelihood.

"You're not going to hurt me," she said. And she searched those eyes for something. All right, he'd said that he wasn't good. But she had a feeling that he was honest. Otherwise, there would have been no reason for him to tell her he wasn't good, except to hit back at her, and she had a feeling that wasn't it. That wasn't why.

There was more to it than that.

Somehow she knew that if she asked this question, he would answer. Even if the answer was yes, he was going to hurt her. He had no reason to lie to her, that was the thing. She was at his mercy and he knew it.

"No," he said. "I swear to you that no harm will come to you. My brother intends to make you his bride, not his slave. And as far as I go… I'm your protector, Violet, not your enemy. I have been charged with transporting you back to Monte Blanco and if I were to allow any harm to come to you, you can rest assured that my brother would see me rotting in my father's favorite dungeon."

"Your father had a favorite dungeon?"

"More than one, actually."

"Wow."

She didn't know why she felt mollified by his assurance that he wouldn't hurt her. Especially not considering he had just said his father had a favorite dungeon. But he made it clear that he and his brother weren't like their father. So if she could believe that…

It was insane that she believed him. But the thing was, he hadn't lied to her. Not once. Her father had tricked her. Had made her believe that the life she was living was different than the one she actually had. That their relationship was different.

But this man had never lied.

Her world felt turned upside down, and suddenly, her kidnapper seemed about the most trustworthy person.

A sad state of affairs.

The car halted on the tarmac, and there was a plane. It didn't look like a private charter, because it was the size of a commercial jet.

But the royal crest on the side seemed to indicate that it was in fact his jet.

Or his brother's. However that worked.

"This way," he said, getting out of the limousine and holding the door for her.

The driver had gotten out and stood there feebly. "I think he was going to hold the door," she said, looking up at Javier.

Her heart scampered up into her throat as her eyes connected with his again. Looking at him was like getting hit with a force. She had never experienced anything quite like it.

It wasn't simply that he was beautiful—though he was—it was the hardness to him. The overwhelming feeling of rampant masculinity coming at her like a testosterone-fueled train.

Admittedly, she was not exposed to men like him all that often. Not in her line of work.

She actually hadn't been certain that men like him existed.

Well, there was her brother-in-law, Dante, who was a hard man indeed, but still, he looked approachable in comparison to Javier.

This man was like a throwback from a medieval era. The circumstances of her meeting him—the ones where she was being sold into marriage pit debt—certainly contributing to this feeling.

"Too bad for him," Javier shot back. "I don't wait."

And that, she concluded, was her signal to get out of the limo. She decided to take her time. Because he might not wait, but she did not take orders.

And if she was going to retain any kind of power in the situation, she had better do it now. Hoard little pieces of it as best she could, because he wasn't going to give her any. No. So she would not surrender what she might be able to claim.

"Good to know." She made small micro-movements, sliding across the seat and then flexing her ankles before her feet made contact with the ground. Then she scooted forward a bit more, put her hands on her knees.

And he stood there, not saying anything.

She stood, and as she did so, he bent down, and her face came within scant inches of his. She forgot to breathe. But she did not forget to move. She pitched herself forward and nearly came into contact with the asphalt. He wrapped his arm around her waist and pulled her back against him. Her shoulder blades came into stark contact with his hard chest. It all lasted only a moment, because he released her and allowed her to stand on her own feet as soon as she was steady. But she could still feel him. The impression of him. Burning her.

"If I walk on my own two feet to the airplane, it is not a kidnapping, is it?"

"I'm certainly not married to the narrative of it being a kidnapping. Call it whatever you need to."

She straightened her shoulders and began to walk toward the plane.

Toward her doom.

Violet didn't know which it was.

But she did know that she was going to have to find her control in this, one way or another.

Even if it were only in the simple act of carrying *herself* aboard the plane.

CHAPTER THREE

JAVIER STUDIED THE woman sitting across from him. Her rage had shrunk slightly and was now emanating off her in small waves rather than whole tsunamis.

She had not accepted a drink, and he had made a show of drinking in front of her, to prove that no one was attempting to poison her, or whatever she seemed to imagine.

He was going to have to have words with Matteo once he arrived in Monte Blanco. "You might want to lower your shields," he said.

"Sure," she said. "Allow me to relax. In front of the man who is holding me against my will."

"Remember, you walked on your own two feet to the airplane, which you felt was the difference between a kidnapping and an impromptu vacation."

"It's a kidnapping," she said. "And I'll have some champagne."

"Now that you've watched me drink a glass

and a half and are satisfied that I'm not going to fall down dead?"

"Something like that."

"Why are you in a temper now when you were fine before?"

"This is absurd. I haven't been able to check my social media for hours."

"Is that a problem for you?"

"It's my entire business," she said. "It's built off that. Off connectivity. And viral posts. If I can't make posts, I can't go viral."

"That sounds like something you would want to avoid."

"You're being obtuse. Surely you know what *going viral* means."

"I've heard it," he said. "I can't say that I cared to look too deeply into it. The internet is the least of our concerns in Monte Blanco."

"Well, it's one of my primary concerns, considering it's how I make my living. All fine for you to be able to ignore it, but I can't."

"Also not going to allow you to post from the plane. Anyway. We don't have Wi-Fi up here."

"How do you not have Wi-Fi? Every airplane has that."

"My father didn't have it installed. And my brother has not seen the use for it."

"I find that hard to believe. He's running a country."

"Again. That is not a primary concern in my country. You may find that we have different priorities than you."

"Do you have electricity?" she asked, in what he assumed was mock horror.

"We have electricity."

"Do you live in a moldering castle?"

"It's quite a bit less moldering than when my brother took the throne. But it is a bit medieval, I'm not going to lie."

"Well. All of this is a bit medieval, isn't it?"

"I felt it was quite modern, given you weren't traded for a pair of sheep."

"No. Just my father's gambling debt, extracted from him when he was drunk. What kind of man is your brother that he would do that?"

"I would say honorable. But his primary concern is the country, and while I don't know what his ultimate plans are for you, or why he wants you specifically, I do know there is a reason. One thing I know about him is that he has his reasons."

"Woof," she said.

In spite of himself, amusement tightened his stomach. And that was the last thing he expected to feel at her insolence. She had no idea who he was. He was a weapon. A human blade.

And she... She taunted him.

He was used to women reacting to him with awe. Sometimes they trembled with fear, but in a way that they seemed to enjoy. He was not blind to the effect he had on women. No indeed. He was a powerful man. A man with a title. A man with wealth.

He commanded a military.

Violet King did not tremble with fear when she looked at him.

He took a champagne glass from the table next to him and poured her a measure of liquid, reaching across the space and handing it to her. She didn't move.

"You'll have to come and get it. Contrary to what you may have heard, I don't fetch or deliver."

She scowled and leaned forward, grabbing hold of the glass and clutching it to her chest as she settled back in her chair.

She looked around the expansive airplane. "Do you think this thing is a little bit big?"

"I've never had any complaints."

Color mounted in her cheeks. "Well. Indeed." She downed half the glass of champagne without taking a breath. "I really do wish there was an internet connection."

"But there isn't. Anyway, we left your phone back in your office."

She looked truly panicked at that. "What if somebody else gets a hold of it? I can't have anybody posting on my social media who wasn't approved."

"Such strange concerns you have. Websites. You know, I've been fighting for the life and health of my people for the last several years. I can't imagine being concerned that somebody might post something on a website in my name."

"Optics," she snapped.

"Optics are no concern of mine. I'm concerned with reality. That which you can touch and see. Smell. Feel. That is my concern. Reality."

"It's no less real. It changes people's lives. It affects them profoundly. I built an entire business off of influence."

"You make a product. I did a cursory amount of research on you, Violet. You don't simply post air."

"No. But for want of that air my products wouldn't sell. It's what exposes me to all those people. It's what makes me relevant."

"I should hope that more than a piece of code floating out in cyberspace would make you relevant."

Her lips twitched and she took another sip of champagne. "I'm not going to argue about this with a man who thinks it's perfectly reasonable to bundle me up and take me back to his country."

"I didn't say it was reasonable," he said. "Only that it was going to be done."

After that, they didn't speak.

Upon arrival in Monte Blanco, Javier parted with Violet and made a straight path for his brother's office.

"I've returned," he said.

"Good," Matteo said, barely looking up from his desk. "I assume you have brought the woman with you?"

"Yes. As promised."

"I knew I could count on you. Did she come quietly?"

He thought of the constant barbs that he had been subjected to on the trip.

"No. She is *never* quiet."

Matteo grimaced. "That could be a problem."

"Your Highness."

Javier turned around at the sound of the breathy voice. Matteo's assistant, Livia, had come into the room. She was a small, drab creature, and he had no idea why his brother kept her on. But Matteo was ridiculously attached to her.

"Yes," Matteo said, his voice gentling slightly.

"It's only that the United Council chief called, and he is requesting the presence of Monte Blanco at a meeting. It's about your inclusion."

This was something his brother had been waiting for. His father had stayed out of international affairs, but it was important to both Matteo and Javier that Monte Blanco have a voice in worldwide matters.

"Then I shall call him."

"I don't know that that will be necessary. He only wishes to know if you will accept his invitation to come to the summit this week."

"Well, I'm a bit busy," Matteo said, gesturing toward Javier.

"Oh?" she asked.

"Yes," he responded. "Javier has brought my bride to me."

Livia's eyes widened, but only for a moment. "Of course." That slight widening was the only emotional reaction given by the assistant. But Javier knew how to read people, and he could see that she was disturbed.

He could also see that his brother did not notice. "It is of no consequence," he said. "We must attend. Javier, you will make sure that Violet acclimates while I'm gone."

"Of course," he said. What he did not say was that he was not a trained babysitter for spoiled socialites, but a soldier. Still, he thought it.

"See that my things are collected immediately," Matteo said, addressing Livia. "All the details handled."

He spoke in such incomplete sentences to the woman, and yet she scurried to do his bidding, asking for no clarification at all.

"Don't you think this is a bit outlandish, even for you?"

"My mouse will have no trouble taking care of things," he said, using his nickname for Livia.

"Yes. I forgot. She is your mouse, living only to do as you ask. Though your appalling treatment of your assistant was not actually what I was referring to. That you had me drag this woman across the world, and you will not be in residence."

"It's perfect," he said. "A more traditional sort of relationship, yes? Hearkening back to the days of old. We won't meet until the wedding."

"You forget, she's an American. A thoroughly modern one."

"*You* forget: she has no choice."

"Why exactly do you want Violet King? That's something that I don't understand."

"Because we need to modernize. Because we need to change the way that the world perceives Monte Blanco."

"I was told by your fiancée that the world does not perceive it at all."

"A blessing," Matteo said. "Because if the world did have a perception of us before now, it would not be a good one."

"And you want to change that." He thought of everything Violet had said to him regarding the internet. "Why don't you have Wi-Fi on your plane?"

Matteo blinked. "What does that have to do with anything?"

"Violet seemed to find it odd that you didn't. I told her you weren't concerned with such things. But it appears that you are."

"Well, I've never needed it in the air."

"Your future bride would want it. Otherwise I think she will find traveling with you onerous."

"I didn't realize you would be so concerned for her comfort."

"Well, you put her comfort in my charge."

"And I leave it to you now." Matteo stood from behind the desk. "I understand that it's not ideal, but I know that you'll also trust me when I tell you this is necessary."

"I know," Javier said. "You never do anything that isn't."

"I'm not our father," Matteo said, and not for the first time Javier wondered if he was telling him or telling himself.

He was well familiar with that internal refrain. He knew his brother walked a hard road, but a different one than Javier did.

Javier had been part of his father's army.

Under Javier's oversight, missions had been carried out that had caused harm. He had believed, fully and completely, that he was in the right.

Until one day he'd seen the truth. Seen what love and loyalty had blinded him to.

And he had learned.

That a man could be a villain and not even know.

That with the right lie, a man could commit endless atrocities and call it justice.

"I know," Javier repeated. "You have spent all these past years defying him. I hardly thought that a little bit of power was going to corrupt you entirely."

"But I must be on guard against it. I understand that you may think it medieval for me to force the girl into marriage…"

Javier shrugged. "I have no thoughts on it one way or the other." And it was true. He knew that Violet was unhappy with the situation, but her happiness was not his concern.

Swaths of unhappiness had been cut through his country for decades, and he and his brother were working as hard as they could to undo it. If Matteo thought that making Violet his queen would help with the situation, then it was collateral damage Javier was willing to accept.

"You say that," Matteo said. "But I have a feeling that you always have thoughts."

"Are they relevant, My King?"

"I told you, I am not our father. But for the fact that I'm a few years older than you, you would be King. Or, if I were dead."

"Stay alive," Javier said. "I have no desire to bear the burden of the crown."

"And yet, the burden is heavy enough that I daresay you can feel the weight of it. It is not like you are immune to the responsibilities we face."

"What is the point of sharing blood with our father if we don't do everything, to the point of spilling it, to correct his wrongs?"

"No point at all," Matteo said, nodding. "I must go check on my mouse's progress."

"You call her that to her face?"

"Yes. She finds it endearing."

He thought back to the stricken look on Livia's face when Matteo had mentioned his fiancée. But Javier also thought of the slight note of warmth in his brother's voice when he said it. *Mouse.* He didn't say it as if she were small or gray, though in Javier's opinion she was both. No, he said it as if she were fragile. His to care for.

"She may."

"No. It is because of how I found her. Shivering and gray, and far too small. Like a mouse."

Javier was not certain that Livia liked to be reminded of her origins. However much Matteo might find his name for her affectionate. He meant what he had said to Violet. Javier was not a good man. Matteo might be, but for the two of them it was more honor than it was anything quite so human as goodness.

In fact, the only real evidence Javier had ever seen of softness in his brother was the presence of Livia in the palace. He didn't know the full story of how he had come into... Possession of her, only that he had found her in quite an unfortunate situation and for some reason had decided it was his responsibility to fix that situation.

"You will keep things running while I'm gone," Matteo said, a command and not a question.

"Of course I will."

"And I will endeavor to make sure these meetings go well. You remember what I told you."

"Of course. If ever you were to exhibit characteristics of our father, it would be better that you were dead."

"I meant that."

"And I would kill you myself."

His brother smiled and walked forward clasping his forearm, and Javier clasped his in return. "And that is why I trust you. Because I believe you would."

They were blood brothers. Bonded by blood they hated. The blood of their father. But their bond was unshakable and had always been. Because they had known early on that if they were ever going to overcome the evil of their line, they would have to transcend it.

And they could only do that together.

Their relationship was the most important thing in Javier's life. Because it was the moral ballast for them both. Because Javier knew how easy it was to upset morality. How emotion could cloud it.

How it could cause pain.

Whether he understood Matteo's being so intent to marry Violet or not, he would sup-

port it. All that mattered was Monte Blanco.
Violet's feelings were a nonissue.

All that mattered was the kingdom.

CHAPTER FOUR

VIOLET HAD BEEN essentially born into money. So she was used to grandeur. She was used to the glittering opulence of sparkling shows of wealth. But the palace and Monte Blanco were something else entirely.

It wasn't that the walls were gilded—they were entirely made of gold. The floor, obsidian inlaid with precious metals, rubies and emeralds. The doorframes were gold, shot through with panels of diamond.

Given what Javier had said about the limo, she was somewhat surprised to see such a glaring display of wealth, but then she imagined the palace had been standing for centuries. She could feel it. As if it were built down into the mountain.

And it was indeed on a mountain. Made of white granite, likely the namesake of the country.

It reminded her of Javier himself. Imposing,

commanding, and entirely made of rock. The view down below was… Spectacular.

A carpet of deep, dense pines swooping down before climbing back upward to yet more mountains. She could barely make out what she thought might be a city buried somewhere in there, but if it was, it was very small. The mountains loomed large, fading to blue and purple the farther away they were. Until they nearly turned to mist against the sky. A completely different color than she had ever seen before. As if it were more ice than sky.

She had not thought it would be cold, given that she didn't think of cold when she thought of this region, but nestled as it was between France and Spain at such a high elevation, it was shockingly frigid and much more rugged than she had thought.

Queen of the wilderness. He had brought her out here to be Queen of the wilderness.

The thought made her shiver.

Then she turned away from the view and back toward the bedroom she had been installed in by a helpful member of staff, and she couldn't think of wilderness at all. It was ornate to the point of ridiculousness.

The bed was made of gold. The canopy was comprised of layers of fabric, a glittering and a gauzy layer, with heavy brocade beneath. The covers were velvet, rich purple and gold.

It made the clean, modern lines of her all-white apartment stark in her memory.

She wasn't going to waste time pondering the room, though. What she needed to do was figure out how to talk the King out of this ridiculous idea that they needed to get married. First, she needed to figure out what his motives were. Obviously if he were crazed by lust where she was concerned, there wasn't much she could offer him. At least, nothing much that she was willing to offer.

Violet knew that no one would believe it if she told them, but she had no physical experience with men. She had never been carried away on a tide of passion, and she fully intended to be carried away on a tide of passion when she allowed a man to... Do any of that.

The problem was, she had met so many kinds of men in her life. Hazard of being well connected and well traveled. She had met rich men. Talented men. Actors, chefs, rock stars. CEOs.

Javier is the first prince you ever met...

Well. That didn't matter. The point was, she'd been exposed to a variety of powerful men early on, and inevitably she found them to be... Disappointments.

They either revealed themselves to be arrogant jerks with overinflated opinions of themselves, secret perverts who had only been pretending to listen to her while they contemplated making a move on her, or aggressive nightmares with more hands than a centipede and less sense.

And she had just always thought there could be more than that. More than shrugging and giving in to a wet kiss that she hadn't wanted anyway.

The richer she had become, the more men had seemed to find her a challenge. Whether she was actually issuing one or not.

And that had made her even more disenchanted with them.

And she hadn't held out for passion for all this time to just...

To just be taken by some king that she didn't even know.

She could Google him if she had any devices. But there was no damned internet in this place.

The first active business would be to find out what he wanted. Because she had a lot. She was a billionaire, after all. And, she was well connected. He could break off a chunk of this castle, and it would probably equal her net worth, so there was that. But there had to be something. There had to be. Otherwise, it wouldn't matter if it was her.

Which brought her back to sexually obsessed. Which really creeped her out.

There was a knock on the chamber door, and she jumped. "Come in."

She expected it to be the same woman who had led her to her room, but it wasn't. It was Javier. And when he came in he brought with him all of the tension that she'd felt in her chest the entire time they were together on the plane ride over.

"I wasn't expecting you," she said.

"What were you expecting exactly?"

She realized there was no point in being difficult. Because Javier might be the key to this. "Where is your brother?"

"Eager to see him?"

"No," she said, and she found that was honest. Better the devil she knew, after all. Even if said devil was as unyielding as a rock face. "Did he tell you why he wants to marry me?"

She needed to know. Because she needed to formulate a plan. She needed to get some power back. Or, rather than getting it back, needed to get some of it in the first place.

"Yes," Javier said.

He just stood there. Broad, tall and imposing.

"Would you care to share with the class?"

"I don't think it matters."

"You don't get that it matters to me why this stranger wants to marry me? I would like to know if it has to do with him harboring some sort of obsession for my body."

That made him laugh. And it offended her. "No. My brother has no designs on your body. He thinks that you will be useful in improving the world's view of Monte Blanco. It is in fact his sole focus. Which is what I came to tell you. He is not here."

"He's not here?"

"No. He has gone to the United Council summit. It is very important to him that Monte Blanco be granted inclusion into the Council. For too long, we have been without the benefit of allies. For too long, we have not had a say in how the world works. And it is something my brother feels is key to bringing us into the twenty-first century."

"So he wants my… Influencer reach?"

That was ridiculous. But she could work with that. "He wants me to make the country look better."

"Yes," Javier said.

"Well. That's easy. I can do that without marrying him."

"I'm not sure that's on his agenda."

"Well, then I'll just have to convince him

that it's a better agenda. I'm very convincing. I entered a very crowded market, and I managed to essentially dominate it. You know that I'm the youngest self-made billionaire in the world?"

"Yes," Javier said. "We did in fact look at the basic headlines about you."

"Then he should know that I'll be of much more use to him as a business consultant."

"You sell makeup," he said.

She bristled. "Yes. And I sell it well. Enough that he seems to have taken notice of the impact that I've made on the world. So don't belittle it." She huffed a breath. "Anyway. All I need is a chance to get to know the country."

"Excellent. I'm glad that you think so. Because I believe that my brother's mouse is making an agenda for while they are away."

"His what?"

"His assistant. We have assignments for while he is away. And I am to oversee."

"Are you *babysitting* me?"

"In a sense."

"You know," she said, keeping her voice carefully deadpan. "I seem to recall a Saint Bernard that acted as Nana in a classic cartoon…"

"Don't push it. I can always tell him you met with an unfortunate accident."

"You said you wouldn't hurt me," she said, meeting his gaze, keeping her eyes as stern as possible.

He inclined his head. "So I did."

"Are you a man of your word, Javier?"

"I am."

The simple confidence in those words made her stomach tighten. "Somehow I knew that."

His eyes narrowed. "How?"

She shrugged. "I don't know. I'm a good judge of character, I think. I was born into wealth, and I will tell you that it's an easier life than most. But I had access to... Anything. Any excess that I wanted. Any sort of mischief that I might want to get into. Drugs and older men and parties. People were always after me to do favors for them. And I had to learn very quickly who my real friends might be. Because let me tell you... What people say and what they do are two very different things. Words don't mean anything if they're not backed up by actions."

"Well, I've kidnapped you. What does that action tell you?"

"I didn't think we were going with *kidnap*?"

"That was your call, not mine."

"Well, you're loyal to your brother. I also think you're loyal to... Your own sense of honor. You might say that you aren't good. But you have a moral code. And even if it does extend to allowing you to kidnap me if your brother says it's the right thing to do, I do not think it would ever extend to hurting someone who couldn't defend themselves against you."

He inclined his head. "Fair enough. My father enjoyed inflicting pain upon the weak. He enjoyed exploiting his power. I have no desire to ever involve myself in such a thing. It is an act of cowardice."

"And you're not a coward," she said confidently. "And I think that you might even want to help me prove to your brother that I don't need to marry him so that I can get back to my real life."

"That's where you're wrong. I genuinely don't care about your plan. Not one way or the other. Happiness, in that fleeting immediate sense, is quite immaterial to me. What matters is the greater good. If my brother feels the greater good is served by marrying you, then that is the goal I will help him accomplish. Not what will make you… Happier. As you said, you had a happier life than most. Drugs, parties and rich men, from the sounds of things."

"But I had none of those things," she said, not sure where she had lost the conversation. "It's just that I had access to them. I haven't experienced them. I have too much to live for. Too much experience to explore."

"It seems to me that you had ample opportunity to do so prior to your engagement to my brother."

"I am not engaged. I am *kidnapped*, as you just stated."

"Walked onto the plane with your own two feet, I think you mean."

"You were the one that introduced *kidnap* again."

"You're the one who seems hung up on the terminology."

"I'll prove it. I'll prove that we don't need marriage."

"Fantastic. Feel free. In the meantime, I will set about to fulfill the items on my brother's list. Because that is all I care about."

He turned and began to walk away from her. "Do you have any feelings about anything?"

When he turned back to face her, his eyes were blank. "No."

"You must be a great time in bed," she shot back, not sure where that came from. Except she knew it made men angry when you called their prowess into question, and if she couldn't elicit sympathy from him, then she would be happy to elicit some rage.

"Thankfully for you," he said, his tone hard,

"my bedroom skills will never be a concern of yours. You are not meant for me."

And then he was gone. Leaving her in the oppressive silence created by those thick, wealth-laden walls.

And she had a feeling that for the first time in her life she might have bitten off more than she could chew.

Except, it wasn't even her bite. It was her father's. And she was the one left dealing with it.

CHAPTER FIVE

HER WORDS ECHOED in his head all through the next day, and when he finally received the memo from his brother's assistant, his irritation was at an all-time high. Because what Violet King thought about him in bed was none of his concern. She had an acerbic tongue, and she was irritating. Beautiful, certainly, but annoying.

Had he been the sort of man given to marriage, she would not be the woman that he would choose. But then, marriage would never have to be for him. He didn't have to produce heirs.

He charged down the hall, making his way to her room, where he knocked sharply.

"Don't come in!"

"Why not?"

"I'm not decent."

"Are you undressed?" The image of Violet in some state of undress caused his stomach to tighten, and he cursed himself for acting like an untried boy. She was just a woman.

"No," she said.

He opened the door without waiting for further explanation. And there she sat, at the center of the massive bed looking...

Scrubbed clean.

She looked younger than when he had first seen her yesterday, than she did in any picture he had ever seen.

Her lashes were not so noticeable now, shorter, he thought. Her face looked rounder, her skin softer. Her lips were no longer shiny, but plump and soft looking. Her dark hair fell around her shoulders in riotous waves.

"I don't have my makeup," she said.

He couldn't help it. He laughed. He couldn't remember the last time he had felt actual humor. Until now. The woman was concerned because she did not have her makeup.

"And that concerns me why?"

"It's my... It's my trade. I don't go out without it. It would be a bad advertisement."

"Surely you don't think you need all of that layered onto your face to make you presentable?"

"That's not the point. It's not about being presentable, or whatever. It's just... It's not who I am."

"Your makeup is who you are?"

"I built my empire on it. On my look."

"Well. No one is here to see your look. And we have assignments."

"Assignments?"

"Yes. First, time to give you a tour of the palace. Then we are to discuss your... Appearance."

She waved a hand in front of her face. "I have been discussing my appearance this entire time."

"Well. I don't mean that, precisely. Your role as Queen will require a different sort of... A different sort of approach."

"I'm sorry. I've made it very clear that I'm not on board with this whole Queen thing, and you're talking about how you're going to change my appearance?"

"I'm only telling you what's on the list. We also need to go over customs, expectations. Ballroom etiquette."

"Don't tell me that I'm going to have to take dancing lessons."

"Precisely that."

"This is... *Medieval*."

"Tell me what it is you need from home, and I will accommodate you." Looking at the stubborn set of her face, he realized that he could drag her kicking and screaming into completing these tasks, or he could try to meet her in the middle. Compromise was not exactly second nature to him, but sometimes different tactics were required for dealing with different enemies.

He and his brother had been covert by necessity when dealing with their father. He could certainly manage a bit of finesse with one small makeup mogul.

"I... Well, I need all my beauty supplies. I might be able to come up with a queen-level look using my makeup, but nobody's doing it but me."

"We'll see."

"I can't wear someone else's products." She was verging on melodrama and he would not indulge it in the least if it weren't for his brother.

That was all.

"My concern is not centered on your business. And anyway, yours shouldn't be at this point either."

"Untrue. My primary concern is my business, because I think it's what I have to offer here."

"Why don't we discuss this over breakfast."

"I told you. I can't go out looking like this."

He pushed a button on the intercom by the

door. Moments later the door opened, and in came breakfast for two.

"Oh," Violet said.

"You keep introducing issues that are not issues for me."

She looked deflated. "Fine. I don't actually care about my makeup."

"Then why exactly are you protesting?"

"Because. I want to win. And I figured if you thought I was this ridiculous and unable to function without a full face of makeup, you might send me back."

"Again. Whether or not you become the next Queen of Monte Blanco is not my decision. So you can go ahead and try to make me believe that you are the silliest creature on planet Earth, but it still won't change what's happening."

He moved the cart closer to her bed. She peered down at the contents. "Is that avocado toast?"

"It is," he said. "Of course, I'm told that it's quite trendy the world over. It has always been eaten here."

"Fascinating," she said. "I didn't realize that you were trendsetters."

He picked up his own plate of breakfast and sat in the chair next to her bed. Then he poured two cups of coffee. Her interest became yet more keen.

"I'm not going to poison you," he said. "You keep staring at me as if I might."

She scrabbled to the edge of the bed and reached down, grabbing hold of the plate of avocado toast, bringing it onto the comforter.

Her eyes met his and held. A shift started, somewhere deep in his gut. She didn't move. Or maybe it only felt like she didn't. Like the moment hung suspended.

Then her fingers brushed his as she took the cup, color mounting in her face as she settled back in the bed, away from him.

The distance, he found, helped with the tightening in his stomach.

She took a sip and smiled. "Perfect," she said. "Strong."

"Did you sleep well?"

"I slept about as well as a prisoner in a foreign land can expect to sleep."

"Good to know."

"The pea under the mattress was a bit uncomfortable." A smile tugged the edge of her lips.

She was a strange sort of being, this woman. She had spirit, because God knew in this situation, many other people would have fallen apart completely. But she hadn't. She was attempting to needle him. To manipulate him. From calling him a Saint Bernard to pretending she was devastated by her bare face.

And now she was drinking coffee like a perfectly contented cat.

"Why don't you go ahead and say what's on your mind. I can tell you're dying to."

"I will complete your list," she said. "Down to the dancing lessons. But I want you to show me around the country. Not just the palace."

"To what end?"

"I've been thinking. Your brother wants to bring this country into the modern era. Well. I am the poster child for success in the modern era. And I believe that I can bring some of that to you. I can do it without marrying your brother."

"As far as I'm concerned it's not up for negotiation."

"Fine. We'll table that. But I want you to give me the tools to make it a negotiation with him."

"Perhaps," he said, taking a long drag of his own coffee.

"Look. Even if I do marry your brother, you're going to want me to do this."

"He didn't leave orders to do it. I have no personal feelings on the matter."

"If you get your way, I'm going to live here

for the rest of my life," she said, her voice finally overtaken by emotion. "You don't even want me to see the place? Don't you think that I should be able to... Envision what my life will be?"

This was not a business negotiation. Finally. She wasn't playing at being sharp and witty, or shallow and vapid. Not holding a board meeting curled up in her canopy bed. This, finally, was something real.

And he was not immune to it, he found.

"I'll see what I can accomplish."

She picked up her toast and took a bite of it with ferocity. "Well. At least I approve of your food." She set the toast back down on the plate and brushed some crumbs away from her lips.

She managed to look imperious and ridiculous all at once.

He could not imagine his brother wrangling this creature. She was as mercurial as she was mystifying, and Javier had never been in a position where he had to deal with a woman on this level.

When it came to his personal relationships with women, they weren't all that personal. They were physical. Suddenly, he was in an entanglement with a beautiful woman that was all... All too much to do with her feelings.

"Finish your toast," he said briskly. "I will

send a member of staff to escort you downstairs in roughly an hour. And then, it is time we begin your training."

Violet muttered to herself as she made her way down the vast corridor and toward the ballroom. "Begin your training... Wax on. Wax off."

This was ludicrous. And she was beginning to get severely anxious. She had been in Monte Blanco for more than twelve hours. She had not seen the mysterious King—who had vanished off on some errand, if Javier was to be believed—and she didn't seem to be making any headway when it came to talking herself out of her engagement.

But she was the one who had decided she was better off trying to take the bull by the horns, rather than running and hiding in California. She supposed she had to own the consequences of that rash decision, made in anger.

The castle was vast, and even though she had received rather explicit instructions on how to get to the ballroom, she was a bit concerned that she might just end up lost forever in these winding, glittering halls. Like being at the center of a troll's mountain horde. All gems and glitter and danger.

And as she walked into the vast ballroom

and saw Javier standing there at the center, she felt certain she was staring at the Mountain King. She knew he wasn't the King. Javier was acting on his brother's behest; he had said so many times. Except it was impossible for her to imagine that this man took orders from anyone.

It took her a moment to realize there was someone else in the room. A small round woman with an asymmetrical blond haircut and a dress comprised of layers of chiffon draped over her body like petals.

"The future Queen is here," she said excitedly. "We can begin. My name is Sophie. I will be instructing you in basic Monte Blancan ballroom dance techniques."

"They could be anyone's ballroom dance techniques," Violet said. "They would still be completely new to me."

"You say that like it should frighten me," Sophie said. "It doesn't. Especially not with the Prince acting as your partner."

Violet froze. "He dances?" She pointed at him.

"I have been part of the royal family all of my life," he said. "That necessitated learning various customs. Including, of course, ballroom dancing. There is nothing that you will be subjected to over the course of this training that I was not. And a great many things you will be spared."

There was a darkness to that statement that made a tremor resonate inside of her. But before she could respond to it, he had reached his hand out and taken hold of hers, drawing her up against the hardness of his chest.

He was hot.

And her heart stuttered.

And she felt…

She felt the beginnings of something she had read about. Heard about… But never, ever experienced before.

When he looked down at her, for a moment at least, it wasn't nice what she saw there in his dark eyes. No. It was something else entirely.

She looked down at the floor.

"I will start the music. Javier is a very good dancer, and he will make it easy by providing a solid lead."

He was solid all right. And hot. Like a human furnace.

His hand down low on her back was firm, and the one that grasped hers was surprisingly rough. She would have thought that a prince wouldn't have calluses. But he did.

She wondered what sort of physical work he did. Or if it was from grueling workouts. He certainly had the body of somebody who liked to exact punishment on himself in the gym.

Music began to play in the room, an exacting instrumental piece with clear timing. And then she was moving.

Sophie gave instructions, but Violet felt as if her feet were flying, as if she had no control over the movements herself at all. It felt like magic. And she would have said she had no desire to dance like this, in an empty ballroom in a palace that she was being held in, by the man who was essentially her captor, but it was exhilarating.

She hadn't lied to him when she said she had been given the opportunity to indulge in a great many things in life. She had turned away from most of them. They just hadn't appealed.

But this...

Was this the evidence of being so spoiled that it took some sort of bizarre, singular experience to make her feel? No. She didn't think that was it.

She looked up slightly and could see his mouth. There was something so enticing about the curve of it. Something fascinating about it. She spent a lot of time looking at people's features. Using the natural planes and angles, dips and curves on people's faces to think about ways that makeup might enhance them.

But she had never been entranced by a mouth in quite the way she was now.

She licked her own lips in response to the feeling created inside her when she looked up at him. And she felt him tense. The lines in his body going taut. And when she found the courage inside of herself to look all the way up to his eyes, the ice was completely burned away. And only fire remained.

But she didn't feel threatened. And it wasn't fear that tightened her insides. Wasn't fear that made her feel like she might be burned, scorched from the inside out.

She took a breath and hoped that somehow the quick, decisive movement might cover up the intensity of her reaction to him. But the breath got hung up on a catch in her throat, and her chest locked, as she leaned forward. Her breasts brushed against the hardness of his chest and she felt like she was melting.

She swayed, and he seemed to think she was unsteady, because he locked his arm around her waist and braced her against his body. She felt weightless.

And she had the strangest sense of security. Of protection. She shouldn't. This man was her enemy. After the way he had dismissed her suggestions for finding ways of not being forced into marriage, he was her sworn enemy.

But in his arms she was certain that he would never hurt her. And when she looked up into those eyes, she could easily see an image of him in her mind, holding a sword aloft and pressing her against his body, threatening anyone who might try to claim her. Anyone who might try to take her from him.

She was insane.

She had lost her mind.

She never reacted to men like this. Much less men who were just holding her in captivity until they could marry her off to their brothers.

But looking up into his eyes now, looking at that sculpted, handsome face, made it impossible for her to think of that. It made it impossible for her to think of anything. How isolated she was here. How her friends weren't here, her family wasn't here. She didn't even have her phone. She hadn't thought about her phone from the moment she had woken up this morning.

She had gotten up, scrubbed the makeup off her face, discarded her fake eyelashes and seized on the idea to play a ridiculous damsel in distress. Over eyeliner. And see where that got her. She hadn't been able to stomach it. Because it was too ridiculous.

He might have believed it, but she found that her pride had to come into play somewhere.

So that had been her first waking thought. And then he had appeared.

There had been toast.

He had been handsome.

Now he was touching her.

And somewhere in there logic was turned upside down, twisted, then torn in half.

Because somehow she felt more connected, more present with this man, here in isolation, than she could remember feeling at home for a very long time.

But he's not why you're here.

The thought sent such a cold sliver of dread through her, and it acted like a bucket of icy water dropped over her head.

She was being ridiculous however you sliced it. But feeling… Physical responses to him were ludicrous. Not just because he had brought her here against her will, but because he wasn't even the reason she had been brought here.

It was his brother. His brother who she hadn't even met. She hadn't even googled anything about him, because she didn't have the means to do it.

She extricated herself from Javier's hold, her heart thundering rapidly. "I think I got the hang of it," she said.

"You are doing okay," Sophie said. "I wouldn't call it masterful."

"Well, I'm jet-lagged," Violet said. "Or did you not hear that I was forced onto a plane yesterday afternoon and flown from San Diego."

Sophie looked from Violet to Javier. "I admit I didn't know the whole story."

"Forced," Violet said. "I am being forced to marry King Whatever-his-name-is."

"King Matteo," Javier said.

"Are you?" Sophie's face turned sharp.

"She's fine," Javier said. "Cold feet."

"Oh yes, prewedding jitters are a real issue for kidnapped brides."

"You're clearly terrified for your life," Javier said dryly. "You definitely treat me like I might kill you via lack of Wi-Fi at any moment."

"I'm in withdrawal."

"Leave us," Javier said to Sophie.

"Should I?" Sophie asked Violet.

"I'm not afraid of him," Violet said, tilting her chin upward.

Sophie inclined her head and left the room, doing what Javier told her. "You have my employees questioning me."

"Good. Maybe we'll start a revolution."

"I would advise against that."

"If you hear the people sing, you might want

to make a run for it. And make sure you don't have any guillotines lying around."

"If revolution were that simple, I would have engaged in one a long time ago."

"The history books make it look simple enough."

"And full of casualties. My brother and I did our best to work behind the scenes to keep this country from falling apart. We prevented civil war."

"Good for you," Violet said, but she felt somewhat shamefaced now for making light of something that was apparently a very real issue here. And she shouldn't feel guilty, because she was being held here against her will. There was no place for her to be feeling guilty. He should feel guilty. But of course he wouldn't.

"I have work to do," he said.

"I thought you were going to take me into the city," she called after him.

"I have no desire to spend any more time with a spoiled brat."

"Oh, how awful of me. Do I have a bad attitude about being your prisoner?"

"This is bigger than you. Can't you understand that?"

He really thought that she should be able to take that on board. That she should just be willing to throw her life away because he was convinced that his brother thought she would be the best Queen for the country.

The longer she stood there staring at him, the longer she felt the burn of his conviction going through her skin, the more she realized they might as well be from different planets.

It wasn't a language barrier. It was… An *everything* barrier.

He had sacrificed all his life for the greater good. He could not understand why it didn't make sense to her. Why it wasn't the easiest thing in the world to abandon her expectations about her life and simply throw herself on the pyre of the good of many.

"Javier," she said.

His expression became haughty. "You know people don't simply address me by my first name."

"What do they call you?"

"His Royal Highness, Prince Javier of Monte Blanco."

"That's a mouthful. I'm going to stick with Javier."

"Did I give you permission?"

Tension rolled between them, but it was an irritation. She had a terrible feeling she knew what it was. That maybe he had felt the same thing she had when they had been close earlier.

She chose to ignore it.

She chose to poke at him.

"No. But then, did you ask me if I cared to get it?"

"What is it you want, Violet?"

Her throat went dry, and she almost lost her nerve to ask him what she had intended to.

"Do you do anything for yourself?" She decided that since she was already acting against what would be most people's better judgment, she might as well go ahead and keep doing it.

"No," he said. Then a smile curved the edges of his lips. "One thing. But I keep it separate. In general, no. Because that kind of selfishness leads to the sort of disaster my brother and I just saved our nation from."

"But you know that's not the way the rest of the world works."

"The rest of the world is not responsible for the fates of millions of people. I am. My brother is."

"We just don't expect that, growing up in Southern California."

"That isn't true. Because you're here."

"Because of my business," she said.

"And your father," he said. "Because whatever you think, you feel an obligation toward something other than yourself. Toward your father. Your family. You know what it is to live for those that you love more than you love your own self. Magnify that. That is having a country to protect."

Then he turned and left her standing there, and she found that she had been holding her breath. She hadn't even been aware of that.

She looked around the room. She was now left to her own devices. And that meant... That she would be able to find a computer. She was sure of that. And once she had the internet at her disposal, she would be able to figure out some things that she needed to know.

It occurred to her that she could contact home. If her brother had any idea what had happened to her...

She could also contact the media.

But something had her pushing that thought out of her mind. If she needed to. If she needed to, she could make an international incident. But for some reason she believed everything that Javier told her. And since she did, she truly believed that things in their country had been dire, and that he and his brother were working to make them better.

She didn't want to undo that.

So she supposed he was right. She did have some sense of broader responsibility.

But that was why she needed a better idea

of what she was dealing with. Of who she was dealing with. And that meant she was going exploring.

CHAPTER SIX

JAVIER IMMEDIATELY WENT to the gym. He needed to punish his body. Needed to destroy the fire that had ignited in his veins when he had touched Violet King. It was an aberration. He knew he had to turn his desires on and off like a switch.

In his life, it had been a necessity. Sometimes he had to go months without the touch of a woman, when he and Matteo were deep in trying to redirect one of his father's plans from behind the scenes, or when they were actively harboring refugees, helping wrongly convicted citizens escape from prison... Well, sometimes there was no time for sex. When he wanted a woman, he went and found one.

Weekends in Monaco. Paris. Women who had appetites that matched his own. Voracious. Experience to match the darkness that lived inside of him.

And never, ever a woman who was meant for his brother.

He had far too much self-control for this.

Perhaps the issue was he had been too long without a woman.

It had been several months while he and Matteo worked to right the balance of Monte Blanco. And though he did not think they had been entirely celibate—either of them—since his brother had taken the throne, it had left little time for them to pursue personal pleasure.

Javier was feeling it now.

He growled and did another pull-up before dropping down to the floor, his breath coming hard and fast.

And he could still feel the impression of her softness in his arms. He had been in the gym for hours now, and it had not dissipated.

He would find a woman. He would have one flown in.

At this point, he felt deeply uncomfortable finding his pleasure with women in his own country. The power imbalance was too great.

And he was wary of being like his father.

So you're more comfortable lusting after the woman you're holding captive?

No, he was not comfortable with it. It was why he was here.

Because she was in his care, if one could

say that of a captive. And he could so easily… Crush her.

He had harmed people before in the service of his father. A blot on his soul he would never scrub out.

"Oh."

He whirled around and he saw the object of his torment standing there, her mouth dropped open, her eyes wide.

"What the hell are you doing in here?"

"I asked around. They said that you might be in the gym. And I had found a computer, so I found an internal schematic for the palace and… Anyway. I found my way down here."

"A computer?"

"Yes," she said. "You see, conveniently, your staff doesn't know that I'm a prisoner. They all think that I'm here of my own accord. So of course there is nothing wrong setting me up with a computer that has internet. Really. You need to watch me more closely."

He crossed his arms over his bare chest. "I hear no helicopters. So I assume you did not call in the cavalry?"

"No. I figured I would wait for that."

Her eyes skittered down from his face, landed on his chest and held. Color mounted in her face.

He gritted his teeth. It was a dangerous game she was playing. Whether she knew it or not.

"If you have something to say," he said, his temper coming to an end point, "say it. I'm busy."

"I can see that," she said. "Do you suppose you could find a... You don't have a shirt on hand, do you?"

He didn't particularly care if she was uncomfortable. Not given the state of his own physical comfort over the last several hours. "No. And I'm in the middle of a workout. So I won't be needing a shirt after you leave. It would be wasted effort. Continue."

It was only then that he noticed she was clutching a portfolio in her hand.

She was still wearing the simple outfit that had been provided for her by the staff earlier in the day. Her hair was still loose, her face still free of makeup.

It was unconscionable, how attractive he found that.

He was a busy man. And consequently, his needs were simple. When he pursued a woman for a physical relationship, he liked her to be clearly sophisticated.

A very specific, sleek sort of look with glossy makeup, tight dresses and high-heeled shoes.

Obvious.

Because when you were short on time, *obvious* was the easiest thing.

Violet was anything but, particularly now, and yet she still made his blood boil.

Perhaps this was it. The taint of his father's blood coming to the fore. Bubbling up the moment there was a woman in proximity who was forbidden. Who was forbidden to him? No one and nothing. And so what had he done?

What had he done? He had made the forbidden the most attractive thing.

And that was it. It had to be his body creating this situation. Because there was nothing truly special about her.

Except that tongue of hers.

Razor-sharp and quick.

Her bravery in the face of an uncertain future.

He gritted his teeth again. None of those things mattered to him. A woman's personality meant nothing. She would serve his brother well when it came to a choice of bride, provided Matteo could handle the sharper edges of her, that was. But those things, Javier presumed, would make her a good queen.

When it came to a bedmate… No. It wasn't desirable at all. A construct. A fabrication.

Brought to him by the less desirable parts of him.

He and his brother had always known those things lurked inside of them.

How could they be of their father and consider themselves immune to such things? They didn't. They couldn't.

And so, Javier had to be realistic about it now.

"I have put together a portfolio. Everything I learned about your country. And the ways in which I think I could help by bringing my business here."

"What do you mean?"

"You used to have manufacturing here. You don't anymore. I do most of my manufacturing in the United States, but with products coming to Europe… I don't see why I couldn't have some of it manufactured here. In fact, I think it would be a good thing. It would allow me to keep costs down. And it would bring a substantial amount of employment to your country."

"We are not impoverished."

"No. But particularly the women here are underemployed. Child marriages are still happening in the more rural villages. I know your father looked the other way…"

"Yes," he said, his teeth gritted. "We fought to stop that. We did not look the other way."

"I know. And I know you're still fighting for it. Again. I did a lot of reading today. I feel like I understand… More of what you're trying to do here. Well. I believe in it. And you're right. It doesn't do us any good to live a life to serve only ourselves. And that has never been my goal. Don't you know I have a charity with my sister, for women who are abused?"

He shook his head. "I regret that I do not."

"My sister… She ended up raising her best friend's baby after her friend's ex-lover murdered her. My sister has always been so regretful that she couldn't do more. And so the two of us established a foundation in her honor. I've been looking for more ways to help vulnerable women. Minerva inspired me." She blinked. "I did work only for myself for a while. To try and make my father…" She shook her head. "It doesn't matter. Working on this charity has made me feel better about myself than anything else ever has. Making Monte Blanco my European base will bring an entirely new light to the country."

"You think very highly of yourself."

She shook her head. "No. But I do know a lot about public perception. And I'm very good with it. Gauging it, manipulating it, I suppose. If you want to call it that. I can help."

"Well. I don't think Matteo would be opposed to that."

"I know he wouldn't. And what does he think, anyway? That he could just put me on ice here until he gets back?"

Javier laughed. "I guarantee you he thinks exactly that."

"I'm to believe that he is the softest, most compassionate ruler this country has ever known?"

Javier nodded. "He is. You may find that hard to believe, but it's true."

"I have a question for you."

"Why bother to let me know? You don't seem to have any issue saying exactly what you think or asking for exactly what you want to know."

"All right. So tell me this. How did you know that what your father was doing was wrong? And what inspired you to try to fix it? How did you see outside of the way you were raised? Because a few hours ago when you were facing me down, I realized something. We were not speaking the same language. We expect different things. Because of our realities. For you... Caring about this entire nation of people is part of you the same as breathing. But it wasn't for your father. You weren't taught this... How did you know it?"

It was something he would have wondered, had the memory not been so emblazoned in his mind.

"The answer is the same as it always is. The moment you see the world outside of the little bubble you're raised in, is the moment you stop believing that your perspective is infallible. It is the moment that you begin to question whether or not your reality is in fact the true reality of the world. It was a child marriage. I was newly in the military. Sixteen years old. I happened upon a village. A six-year-old girl was being married off, and she was terrified."

Even now the memory made his teeth set on edge. Made him burn for blood.

"I put a stop to it. Rallied the military, ordered them to hold her father and the groom captive. I remember picking the child up. She was terrified. When I went to my father and told him I was appalled to see that these things were still happening in our country... He scolded me. He said it was not up to me to impose my beliefs on our citizens. My father was no great believer in liberty, Violet. His motivations were related to money. Peace, border protection. Not freedom." He stared hard against the back wall of the gym. "The minute I knew that was the minute that I stopped believing what I saw. It didn't take me long to realize my brother was in a similar crisis of faith. And that was when the two of us began to work to affect change."

"It's amazing," she said. And somehow, he truly believed her. He had never felt particularly amazing. Only like a grim soldier carrying out marching orders that he had never received. But the ones that should have existed. If their leader had had any integrity.

"Most people look away, you know," she said.

"Not me," he said.

"No. Will you please take me out into town?"

"Yes," he agreed.

Because he saw her purpose now. Saw her intent. And because she was correct. It wasn't reasonable for Matteo to keep her here on ice, so to speak.

Anyway, he did not have to check with his brother on every last thing. They had to trust each other. With the way things had been for the past decade and a half, they had no choice. And so, Matteo would have to trust him in this as well.

"Perfect. But I need... I need a phone."

"Your phone, along with your makeup, is

making its way here. You will have it tomorrow. And then I promise you, we will go on your field trip."

"Thank you," she said.

It occurred to him then, the ludicrousness of it all. Of her thanking him when she hated him. Of him standing there, desire coursing through his veins when she was off-limits.

But it didn't matter. Nothing mattered more than Monte Blanco. Nothing mattered more than the good of the nation.

Certainly not his own errant lust.

But tomorrow everything would be as it should be.

He was a man of control. A man of honor.

And he would not forget.

CHAPTER SEVEN

IT HAD TAKEN her several hours to regain her breath after seeing him without his shirt. There it was. She was that basic.

She had known that he was spectacular. Had known that he was muscular and well-built. Because she wasn't blind, and it didn't take a physique detective to know that he was in very good shape underneath those clothes.

But then she had seen it.

His body. All that golden, perfect skin, the dark hair that covered his chest—she would have said that she didn't like chest hair, but apparently she did—and created an enticing line that ran through the center of his abdominal muscles.

He was hot.

Her captor was hot.

She did not have time to ponder that. She had a mission.

She steeled herself and took one last look in

the mirror before leaving her room. She had told him they could meet in the antechamber. She was pretty sure she knew which room the antechamber was. She had made it her business to figure out the layout of the palace. It was difficult. But she had done it.

And she had her phone back.

She had been feeling gleeful about that since the moment it had been deposited into her hand this morning.

And yet... And yet.

She hadn't been able to think of a single thing to update her account with.

If she still didn't want to call home.

Because she was mad.

Because she didn't even know what to say.

She tucked her phone in her purse and made her way to the appointed meeting place. He was already there. She tried to force her eyes to skim over him, not to cling to the hard lines and angles of his body. To the terrifying symmetry of his face.

Terrifying and beautiful.

Saved only by that scar along his cheekbone.

She wanted to know how he got it.

She shouldn't want to know how he got it. She shouldn't want to know anything about him.

"Good morning. As you can see," she said,

waving her hand over her face, "I'm restored to my former glory."

His eyes moved over her dispassionately. And she felt thoroughly dismissed. Insulted.

She shouldn't care.

"All right. Where are we going to first?"

"The capital city. I thought that would be the perfect place to start. It's about thirty minutes away. Down the mountain."

"Excellent."

Her stomach tightened, her hand shaking. And she didn't know if it was because of the idea of being in close proximity with him in a car for that long or if it was stepping outside of this palace for the first time in several days.

The lack of reality in the situation was underlined here. By her containment. In this glittering palace of jewels it was easy to believe it was all a dream. Some kind of childhood fantasy hallucination with the very adult inclusion of a massive, muscular male.

But once they left the palace, the world would expand. And the fantasy that it was a dream would dissolve. Completely.

There was no limousine waiting for them. Instead, there was a sleek black car that was somehow both intensely expensive looking and understated. She didn't know how it accomplished both of those things. But it did.

And it seemed right, somehow, because the car's owner was not understated and could not be if he tried.

Looking at him now in his exquisitely cut dark suit, she had a feeling that he was trying.

That this was the most inconspicuous he could possibly be. But he was six and a half feet tall, arrestingly beautiful and looked like he could kill a hundred people using only his thumb. So. Blending wasn't exactly an option for him.

He opened the door for her, and she got inside.

When he went to the driver's seat, her tension wound up a notch.

It was even smaller than she had imagined. She had thought they might have a driver. Someone to help defuse this thing between them.

Between them. He probably felt nothing. Why would he?

He was carved out of rock.

Well. One thing.

She thought of his response to her question yesterday. The way that his lips had curved up into a smile.

One thing.

The idea of this rock as a sexual being just

about made her combust. She did not need those thoughts. No, she did not.

He was not the kind of man for her. Even in fantasy. She needed a sexual fantasy with training wheels. An accountant, maybe. Soft. One who wore pleated-front khakis and emanated concern. A nice man named Stephen.

The kind of man that would bring her cinnamon rolls in bed.

After... Making tender love to her.

Nothing about that appealed.

She had no idea why her sexuality was being so specific. She had never intended to make it to twenty-six a virgin.

And she had certainly never intended for this man to awaken her desire.

No. It was just exacerbated by the fact that this felt like a dream. That was all. She wasn't connected to reality. And she was... Stockholm syndrome. That was it. She was suffering from sexual Stockholm syndrome.

When the car started moving, she unrolled the window and stuck her head out of it. Breathed in the crystal mountain air and hoped that it would inject her with some sense.

It didn't.

It did nothing to alleviate the bigness of his presence in the tiny vehicle.

"Are you going to roll the window up? Because you know I don't make a habit of driving to public spaces with women hanging out my car."

She shot him a look and rolled the window up. It really did her no good to oppose him now. She was on a mission. Trying to prove something. "I was enjoying the air."

"Now which one of us is a Saint Bernard?"

"Did you just make a joke?" She looked at his stern profile and saw the corner of his lip tip upward. "You did. You made a joke. That's incredible."

"Don't get used to it."

It felt like a deeper warning of something else. But she went ahead and ignored it. Along with the shiver of sensation that went through her body.

They were silent after that. And she watched as the trees thinned, gave way to civilization. The dirt becoming loose rocks, and then cobblestone.

The town itself was not modern. And she would have been disappointed if it was. The streets were made of interlocking stones, the sidewalks the same, only in a different pattern. Tight spirals and sunbursts, some of them bleeding up the sides of the buildings that seemed somehow rooted to the earth.

The streets were narrow, the businesses packed tightly together. There were little cafés and a surprising number of appealing-looking designer shops that Violet suddenly felt eager to explore.

"This is beautiful," she said. "If people knew... Well, if people knew, this would be a huge tourist spot."

"It was not encouraged under the rule of my father. And in these past years businesses have rebounded. But still..."

"There is ground to gain. Understood. Pull over."

"What?"

"Pull over."

She saw a bright yellow bicycle leaned against a wall. And right next to it was a window planter with bright red geraniums bursting over the top of it.

All backed by that charming gray stone.

"We need to take a photo."

He obeyed her, but was clearly skeptical about her intent.

She got out of the car quickly and raced over to the bike. Then she looked over into the courtyard of the neighboring café. People were sitting outside drinking coffee. "Excuse me? Is this your bike?" She asked the young woman sitting there working on her computer.

The woman looked at her warily and then saw Javier, standing behind her. Her eyes widened.

"It's fine," Violet said. "He's harmless. I just want to take a picture with your bike."

"Of course," the woman said.

She still looked completely frazzled, but Violet scampered to where it was, positioning herself right next to it and putting her hand over the handlebars. "A picture," she said. She reached into her purse and pulled her phone out, handing it to him.

"That's what all this is about? Also. I am not harmless."

"Yes. Very ferocious. Take my picture."

She looked straight ahead, offering him her profile, and tousled her hair lightly before positioning her hand delicately at her hip.

"There," he said. "Satisfied?"

"Let me verify." She snatched the phone from his hand and looked at the photo.

It had done exactly what she wanted to do, and with some tweaking, the colors would look beautiful against the simple gray stone.

"Yes," she confirmed. "I am."

She pulled up her account, touched the picture up quickly and typed:

Exploring new places is one of my favorite things. Stay tuned for more information on your next favorite vacation spot.

"There," she said. "That's bound to create speculation. Excitement."

He looked down at the picture with great skepticism. "That?"

"Yes."

"I do not understand people."

"Maybe they don't understand you," she said.

He looked completely unamused by that.

"Sorry. Joke. I thought you were getting to where you understood those sometimes."

The look he gave her was inscrutable.

"Show me the rest of this place," she said. "I'm curious."

He looked at her as if she had grown a second head. "You realize that I'm slightly conspicuous?"

"Usually I am too," she said. "I guess... I just figure you ignore it."

"You're not conspicuous here."

"No," she said. "But that won't last long, will it? I mean, if I'm going to be the Queen..."

"You're not going to be inconspicuous as long as you're walking around with me. That's a pretty decent indicator that you might be important."

"Wow. No points for humility."

"Do you have false humility about the degree to which you're recognized? Or what your status means? You've been throwing all sorts of statistics at me about your wealth and importance ever since we first met."

"All right," she said. "Fair enough."

They walked on in silence for a moment. She paid attention to the way her feet connected to the cobblestones. It was therapeutic in a way. There was something so quaint about this. It was more village than city, but it contained a lot more places of interest than she would normally think you would find in a village.

"What is the chief export here?"

"There isn't any. We are quite self-contained. What we make tends to stay here, tends to fuel the citizens."

"That's very unusual."

"Yes. It also feels precarious."

"So… If we were to manufacture my products here, I would be your chief export."

"In point of fact, yes."

"Though, if your other products became desirable because of tourism…"

"Yes. I understand it would mean a great deal of cash injection for the country. Though, thanks to my brother's personal fortune, the coffers of the country have been boosted as it is."

"Yes, I did some research on him. He's quite a successful businessman."

"You would like him. Other than the fact that he's a bit of a tyrant."

"More than you?"

"Different than me." He relented. "Perhaps not more."

"A family of softies."

The sound he made was somewhere between a huff of indignation and a growl. "I have never been called soft."

She looked at him. The wall of muscle that was his chest. The granite set of his jaw. She meant her response to be light. Funny. But looking at him took her breath. "No. I don't suppose you have."

There was a small ice-cream parlor up the way, and she was more than grateful for the distraction. "I want ice cream," she said.

"*Ice cream?* Are you a child?"

"Ice cream is not just for children," she said gravely. "Surely you know that, Javier."

"I don't eat ice cream."

"Nonsense. Everyone needs ice cream. Well, unless they're lactose intolerant. In which case, they just need to find a good nondairy replacement. And let me tell you, in Southern California they're plentiful."

"I'm not intolerant of anything."

She tried, and failed, to hold back a laugh. "Well, that just isn't true. I've only spent a few days in your company, but I can tell you that you're clearly intolerant of a whole host of things. But, it's good to know that dairy isn't among them."

"You are incredibly irritating."

"*Not* the first time I've heard that."

"And who told you that?"

"My older brother, for a start. Also, my surrogate older brother, Dante. He's now my brother-in-law, incidentally."

"That seems convoluted."

"It's not really. Not at all. Just the way things ended up. My father quite literally found him on a business trip and brought him home. Took care of him. I think my sister was in love with him for most of her life."

"But you weren't."

She laughed. "I remember very clearly telling Minerva that I didn't like men who were quite as hard as Dante."

A tense silence settled between the two of them. She hadn't meant to say that. Because of course that implied that perhaps it had changed. And perhaps there was a hard man that she might find appealing after all.

She gritted her teeth.

"And I still don't," she said. "So. Just so we're both clear."

"Very clear," he said.

"Now. Ice cream." She increased her pace and breezed straight into the shop. And she did not miss the look of absolute shock on the faces of the proprietors inside. It wasn't to do with her. It was to do with Javier.

"I saw that there was ice cream," she said cheerily. She approached the counter and looked at all the flavors.

"We make them all here," the woman behind the counter said, her voice somewhat timid. "The milk comes from our own cows."

"Well, that's wonderful," Violet said. "And makes me even more excited to try it." There was one called Spanish chocolate, and she elected to get a cone with two scoops of that. She kept her eyes on Javier the entire time.

"You don't want anything?"

"No," he said, his voice uncompromising.

"You're missing out," she said.

She went to pay for the treat, and he stepped in, taking his wallet from his pocket.

"Of course we cannot ask Your Royal Highness to pay," the woman said.

"On the contrary," Javier said, his voice decisive. "You should be asking me to pay double. Consider it repayment."

The woman did not charge Javier double, but she did allow him to pay.

"I didn't need you to buy my ice cream," she said when they were out on the street.

"It's not about need. It is about... What feels right."

"You're that kind of man, huh? The kind that holds open doors and pays for dinner?"

He laughed, a dark, short sound. "You make me sound quite a bit more conventional than I am."

"A regular gentleman."

"I would not say that."

"Well, what would you say, then? You're single-handedly setting out to save the country, and you saved a little girl from child marriage. You worked for years to undo the rule of your father." She took a short lick of her ice cream. It was amazing. "I would say that runs toward gentlemanly behavior, don't you?"

"I think that's overstating human decency. I would like to think that any man with a spine would do what I did in my position. Inaction in my position would be complicity. And I refused to be complicit in my father's actions."

"Well. Many people would be, for their comfort."

She looked down the alleyway and saw a lovely hand-painted mural. She darted there, and he followed. It was secluded, ivy growing over the walls, creeping between the brick.

"I just need a picture of this."

She held out her hand, extending her ice-cream cone to him. "Can you hold this?"

He took it gingerly from her grasp, looking at it like it might bite him. She lifted her brows, then turned away from him, snapping a quick picture and then another for good measure.

He was still holding the ice-cream cone and looking aggrieved, so when she returned, she leaned in, licking the ice-cream cone while he held it still.

His posture went stiff.

He was reacting to her, she realized. The same way that she reacted to him. And she didn't like how it made her feel. Giddy and jittery and excited in a way she couldn't remember feeling before.

And she should pull away. She should.

But instead, she wrapped her hand around his, and sent electric sensation shooting through her body.

"You should taste it," she said.

"I told you, I didn't want any."

"But I think you do," she insisted. "You should have some."

She pushed his hand, moving the cone in his direction, and she could see the moment that he realized it was better to take the path of least resistance. He licked the ice cream slowly, his dark eyes connecting with hers.

She realized she had miscalculated.

Because he had his mouth where hers had been.

Because she was touching him and he was looking at her.

Because something in his dark eyes told her that he would be just as happy licking her as he was this ice cream.

And all of it was wrong.

Why couldn't she hate him? She should.

Why couldn't she get it into her head that this was real? That it was insane. That she should want to kick him in the shins and run as far and fast as she could. Call for help at the nearest business, rather than lingering here in an alley with him.

"It's good," she said, her throat dry.

"Yes," he agreed, his voice rough.

Then he thrust it back into her hand. "I think I've had enough."

"Right."

Her heart clenched, sank. And she didn't know what was happening inside of her. Didn't know why her body was reacting this way, now, to him. Didn't know why she felt like crying, and not for any of the reasons that she should.

"I'm not done exploring the city, though. And I wouldn't want to take my ice cream back in your car. I might make a mess."

But the rest of the outing was completely muted. Not at all what it had been before.

And that it disappointed her confused her even more than anything else.

When she was back at the palace, back in her room, she lay down and covered her head. And only then did she allow herself to think the truth.

She was attracted to the man who was holding her captive.

She was attracted to the brother of the man she was being forced to marry.

But more important, he was attracted to her. She had seen it.

She had very nearly tasted it.

Thankfully, they had come to their senses.

She spent the rest of the night trying fitfully to be thankful when all she felt was frustrated.

And she knew that she had come up with a plan, no matter how it made her stomach churn to think of putting it into action.

She had no choice.

CHAPTER EIGHT

HIS BROTHER STILL hadn't returned.

Javier was tired of being tested. He had been avoiding Violet since they had come back from the city the other day. The temptation that she had presented to him was unacceptable.

That he had the capacity to be tempted was not something that he had first seen. But Violet King had tested him at every turn, and the true issue was that he feared he might fail a test if she continued.

He curled his fingers into fists. No. He was not a weak man.

Even before he had turned on his father, he had not had an easy life. He had faithfully served in his father's army. And that had required work guarding the borders in the forests, camping out for long periods of time. His father's paranoia meant that he was certain that enemies were lurking behind every tree.

And Javier had found that to be so. His father had had many enemies. And Javier had done his job in arresting them.

He wasn't sure what he wished to avoid thinking about more. That period of time in his life, or his current attraction to Violet.

"Of course, the architecture is nothing compared to the natural beauty. You got a little peek outside the window, but more to come later on this beautiful vacation spot."

He heard Violet's voice drifting down the corridor, coming from the expansive dining room where his brother often held dinner parties.

It was a massive room with a view that stretched on for miles, a large balcony connecting it and the ballroom and making the most of those views.

Violet was standing right next to the window, her cell phone in her hand. She waved—not at him, but at her screen—then put the phone down at her side. "I was filming a live video. Doing more to tease my location."

"Of course you were," he said.

She gave him a bland look. "Just because you don't understand it doesn't mean it's not valid."

"Oh, I would never think that."

"Liar. If you don't understand it, you think it's beneath you."

"I didn't say I didn't understand it."

"But you do think it's beneath you."

"That was implied in my statement, I think."

"You're impossible."

She walked nearer to him, and he tried to keep his focus on the view outside. But he found himself looking at her. She had most definitely regained her precious makeup. She looked much as she did that first day he had seen her, which he assumed was a signature look for her.

"So you must go to all this trouble," he said, indicating her makeup, "to talk to people who aren't even in the room with you."

She winked. "That's how you know I like you. If I talk to you in the same room, and I don't bother to put my eyelashes on."

"Your eyelashes are fake?"

"A lot of people have fake eyelashes," she said sagely. "I used to have them individually glued on every week or so, but I prefer the flexibility of the strips so I can just take them off myself at the end of the day."

"I have to say I vastly don't care about your eyelashes."

He looked down at her, at the dramatic sweep of those coal black lashes they were discussing. And he found that he did care, more than he would like. Not about the application, but that he wished he could see them naturally as they had been the other morning. Dark close to her eyes, lighter at the tips. He appreciated now the intimacy of that sight.

And he should not want more.

"You know what I do care about?" she asked. "Outside. I would like to go outside."

"Well, the garden is fenced in, feel free to wander around. Just don't dig underneath it."

"Very cute. Another joke. We could write that in your baby book. However, I would like a tour."

"A tour of the grounds?"

"Yes."

"Of the garden, or of the entire grounds? Because I warn you, they are quite wild."

"I find I'm in the mood for wild."

She smiled slightly and enigmatically. He could not tell whether she intended for the statement to be a double entendre.

But the moment passed, and he found himself agreeing to take her out of the palace.

One path led to the carefully manicured gardens that had been tamed and kept for generations. A testament to the might of the royal family, he had always thought. And as a result, he had never liked them.

"This way," he said. "This is where Matteo and I used to play when we were boys."

The rocky path led down to a grove of trees. Heavily shaded, and next to a deep, fathomless swimming hole.

A waterfall poured down black, craggy rocks into the depths.

The water was a crystalline blue, utterly and completely clear. The bottom of the river was visible, making it seem like it might not be as deep as it was. But he knew that you could sink and sink and not find the end of it.

He and Matteo had always loved it here. It had seemed like another world. Somewhere separate from the strictures of the palace. Though, at that point he had not yet come to hate it.

Still. He had appreciated the time spent outdoors with his brother. His brother had been most serious at that age.

Perhaps because he had always known that the burden of the crown would be his.

"This is beautiful," she said. He expected her to reach for her phone immediately, but she didn't. Instead, she simply turned in a circle, looking at the unspoiled splendor around them.

"Yes. You know something? I know that my father never set foot down here." He stared at the pool. "And now he's dead."

"That's a tragedy," Violet said. "To live right

next to something so beautiful and to never see it."

"There were a great many things my father didn't see. Or care about. He cared about his own power. He cared about his own comfort. This is just one of the many things he never truly looked at. Including the pain that he caused his own people."

"But you did. You do," she said.

"For better or worse."

"You used to swim down here?"

"Yes."

"Did you laugh and have fun?"

"Of course I did."

"I can't imagine you having fun."

"I can assure you I did."

"It's safe?" she asked.

"Yes."

She took her phone out of her pocket and set it on the shore. Then she looked back at him and kicked her shoes off, putting her toe in the water. "It's freezing," she said.

"I said it was safe. I didn't say it wasn't frigid water coming down from an ice melt."

She stared at him, a strange sort of challenge lighting her eyes.

"What?"

"Let's swim."

"No," he said.

He realized right then that the outright denial was a mistake. Because her chin tilted upward in total, stubborn defiance. And the next thing he knew she had gone and done it. Gone in, clothes and all, her dark head disappearing beneath the clear surface. And she swam.

Her hair streaming around her like silken ribbon, her limbs elegant, her dress billowing around her. And he was sure that he could see white cotton panties there beneath the surface. He felt punched in the gut by that. Hard.

"Swim with me," she said.

"No."

She swam up to the edge, giving him an impish grin. "Please."

He remembered her words from the other day. *Don't you do anything for yourself?*

He didn't. He didn't, because there was no point.

But swimming wasn't a betrayal.

He could feel his body's response to that in his teeth. A twist in his gut. Because he knew what he was doing. Knew that he was pushing at that which was acceptable.

But the water would be cold.

And he would not touch her. Tension rolled from his shoulders, and he unbuttoned his shirt, leaving it on the banks of the river. His shoes, his pants. And leaving himself in only the dark shorts that he wore beneath his clothes.

Then he dived, clearing her completely, sliding beneath the surface of the water at the center of the pool, letting the icy water numb his skin like pinpricks over the surface of it. Maybe it would knock the desire that he felt for her out of his body.

Maybe.

He swam toward her, and he saw something flash in the depths of her eyes. Surprise. Maybe even fear.

He stopped just short of her.

"Is this what you had in mind?"

"I didn't expect the strip show."

The characterization of what had occurred made his stomach tighten. Or the cold water had no effect on his desire.

He couldn't understand why. Why this woman, at this moment, tested him so.

Any retort she might have made, any continuation of the conversation seemed to die on her lips.

And he knew. He knew that he had just gone straight into temptation. Had literally dived right in. Whatever he had told himself in that moment on the shore was a lie. All he had wanted to do was to be closer to her.

He had never experienced anything like this.

Had never experienced this kind of draw to a woman before. To anyone.

She had nothing in common with him. A spoiled, sheltered girl from the United States. But when she looked at him, he felt something. And he had not felt anything for a long time.

She began to draw closer to him.

"Don't," he said.

"I just…" A droplet of water slid down her face, and her tongue darted out. She licked it off. She reached out and dragged her thumb over the scar on his cheek. "How did you get this?"

Her touch sent a lightning bolt of desire straight down to his groin. "It's not a good story."

"I don't care."

"You think you don't care, but you haven't heard it."

Her hand was still on him.

"Tell me," she insisted.

"You know you should be afraid of me," he said. "And here you are, pushing me."

"You said you wouldn't hurt me."

"And I wouldn't. Intentionally. But you are here touching me as if I cannot be tempted into anything that we would both regret."

"Who says I would regret it?"

He gritted his teeth. "You would."

"Javier…"

"I was helping a man escape from prison. Wrongfully arrested by my father. One of his guards attempted to put a stop to it. It was war, Violet, and I did what had to be done."

She said nothing. She only looked at him, her eyes wide.

"Yes. It is what you think."

"You did what you had to," she said softly.

"But that's what I am. A man who does what he has to. A man who is barely a man anymore."

She slid her thumb across his skin, and he shuddered beneath her touch. "You feel like a man to me," she whispered.

"You are not for me."

He pushed away from her and swam back to the shore. She watched him dress, the attention that she paid him disconcerting. Then she got out of the water, the thin fabric of her dress molded to her curves. He could see her nipples, clearly visible, and his arousal roared.

"You are not for me."

Then he turned, leaving her there. She would find her way back. Follow the path.

But he had to do them both a favor and remove himself from her. Because if he did not, he would do something that they would both come to bitterly regret.

* * *

He was familiar with the sting of failure. The process of deprogramming himself from his father's rule had been a difficult one when he had been sixteen years old and he had wanted to believe with intensity that his father was a benevolent ruler. And he had seen otherwise. The way that it had hurt his soul, torn him in two, to begin to look differently at the world, at his life and at himself, had been the last time he had truly felt pain. Because after that it was over. After that, the numbness had sunk in, had pervaded all that he was.

It was Matteo who had seen him through it. Matteo, who had been struggling with the exact same thing, who made Javier feel like he wasn't losing his mind.

His brother had been his anchor in the most difficult moment of his life.

And now there was another wrenching happening in his soul. It was all because of the luminous, dark eyes of Violet King.

In that alleyway, when she had put her hand over his, when she had tempted him with a bite of ice cream like she was Eve in the garden offering him an apple, he had not been able to think of anything but casting the frozen treat aside and claiming her mouth with his own.

In the water he had longed to drag her to the shore, cover her body with his own. Claim her.

And that was a violation of all that he had become.

He was a man of honor because he had chosen it.

None of it was bred into him. None of it was part of his blood.

He and Matteo knew that, so they were always on guard.

And this woman... This woman enticed him to betray that.

To betray his brother.

The one man to whom he owed his absolute loyalty.

The man he had promised to destroy should that man ever abuse his power. Such was their bond.

Such was his dedication.

But now... Lusting after his brother's fiancée made him compromised.

It compromised that promise. Compromised what he was. What he claimed to be.

His phone rang.

It was Matteo. As if his brother could feel his betrayal from across the continent.

"Yes?"

"We have been successful," Matteo said. "Monte Blanco will now be included in the

United Council. My mouse has proven herself indispensable yet again."

"Is she in the room with you?"

"Of course she is."

Javier didn't even have the right to scold his brother for that. Not at this point. He had lost his right to a moral high ground of any kind.

"When do you return?" he said, his voice heavy.

"Two days. We have to make a stop in Paris for a diplomatic meeting."

"I suppose, then, that it is good you spent all those years studying business."

"Yes. Not the way our father did it, but there are similarities to diplomacy in business and when it comes to running a country. Of course, the bottom line is not filling your own pockets in the situation."

"No indeed."

The bottom line was not about satisfying themselves at all.

It stung particularly now. As he thought of Violet. As he thought of the deep, gut-wrenching longing to touch her.

And the anger that crept in beneath his skin. Anger that was not at himself, though it should have been. Anger at the cruelty of fate. That he should want this woman above all others when she was perhaps the only woman in the world who was truly off-limits to him.

He was a prince. He could snap his fingers and demand that which he wished.

Except her.

The insidious doubt inside of him asked the question. Was that why he wanted her? Was that why she presented a particular appeal? Because she was forbidden.

Because she was forbidden to him and no matter how hard he tried to pretend otherwise, he was born a man with a massive ego who didn't feel that a single thing on the earth should be barred from him should he take to it.

No. He would not allow it.

He would not allow that to be true.

"I look forward to your return."

"How is my fiancée?"

"Not exactly amenable to the idea of being your fiancée," he said.

It was the truth. Everything else could be ignored. For now.

"I must say, the connection between myself and her is one of the things that made our meetings the most interesting. She is well liked, world-renowned for her business mind. Such a fantastic asset to me she will be."

"You don't know her."

"And I suppose you do now. I will look forward to hearing how you think I might best manage her."

His brother hung up then. And left Javier standing there with his hand curled so tightly around the phone he thought he might break. Either his bones or the device, he didn't know. Neither did he care.

He gritted his teeth and walked out of his office. Something compelled him down to the ballroom where he had the dance lesson with Violet. Where he held her in his arms and first began to question all that he was. It was unconscionable. That this woman he had known for a scant number of days could undo twenty years' worth of restraint.

And when he flung open the doors to the ballroom… There she was.

Curled up in one of the tufted chairs that sat in the corner of the room, next to the floor-to-ceiling windows, sunlight bathing her beauty in gold.

Her legs were tucked up underneath her, and he could see the edges of her bare toes peeking out from beneath her shapely rear. She was wearing simple, soft-looking clothes, nothing fancy. Neither did she have on any of her makeup. She was reading.

Not on her phone.

And it made him want to dig deeper. To

question all that she presented of herself to the world, all that she tried to tell him about who she was and who she actually might be.

She looked up when she heard his footsteps. "Oh," she said. "I didn't expect you to be lurking around the ballroom."

"I didn't expect you to be lurking around at all. Much less away from the computer."

"I found this book in the library," she said. "And the library's beautiful, but it doesn't have the natural lighting of this room."

"Protecting the books," he said.

"Makes sense."

"What is it you're reading?"

"It's a book of fairy tales. Monte Blancan fairy tales. It's very interesting. We all have our versions of these same stories. I guess because they speak to something human inside of us. I think my favorite one that I've read so far is about the Princess who was taken captive by a beast."

"Is that what you think me? A beast?"

She closed the book slowly and set it down on the table beside the chair. "Possibly. Are you under some kind of enchantment?"

"No."

"That's something I found interesting in your version of the story. The Prince was not a beast because of his own sins. He was transformed into one as punishment for something his father had done. And then, much like the story I'm familiar with, the woman is taken captive because of the sins of her father. It feels shockingly close to home, doesn't it?"

"Except I believe in the story my brother would be that enchanted Prince."

Her gaze was too frank. Too direct. "If you say so."

"You were shocked by your father's deal?"

She nodded slowly. "I was. Because I thought that we... I knew he wasn't perfect. I did. But it's not like he was a raving villain like your father."

"You know, I didn't realize my father was a raving villain until I started to see, really see the things that he had done to our country. And I don't know that your father is a villain so much as he was made a desperate man in a desperate moment. And my brother took advantage of that. My brother does his best to act with honor. But like me, he is not afraid to be ruthless when he must be. I do not envy the man who had to go up against his will."

"He should have protected me. He should never have used me as currency. I can't get over that. I won't."

"Is that why you came? To teach him a lesson?"

Her lips twitched. "Maybe. And I won't lie, I did think that perhaps my notoriety would keep me safe. You know, because people will miss me if I'm not around. But I sort of like not being around. It's been an interesting vacation."

"Except you're going to marry my brother."

"Yes. I know you think so."

"You can take it up with him when he returns. He tells me he'll be back in two days."

Shock flared in the depths of her eyes. "Two days?"

"Yes. Don't look so dismayed."

"I can't help it. I am dismayed."

"Why exactly?"

"I just thought there was more time."

There was something wild in the depths of her eyes then, and he wanted to move closer to it. But he knew that would be a mistake. Still, when she stood, it was to draw closer to him.

"I know that you feel it," she said. "It's crazy, isn't it? I shouldn't feel anything for you. But you… I mean, look, I know it's chemistry, or whatever, I know it's not feelings. But…" She bit her full lower lip and looked up at him from beneath her lashes, the expression both innocent and coquettish. "Don't you think that maybe we should have a chance to taste it before I'm sold into marriage?"

"I thought you were intent on resisting that," he said, his voice rough.

"With everything I have in me."

"I cannot. I owe my brother my undying loyalty. And I will not compromise that over something as basic as sex. You mistake me, *querida*, if you think that I can be so easily shaken."

"I know that you're a man of honor. A man of loyalty. But I feel no such loyalty to your brother. And it is nothing to me to violate it."

She planted her hand on his chest. And he knew that she could feel it then. Feel his heart raging against the muscle and blood and bone there. Feel it raging against everything that was good and right and real, that which he had placed his faith in all these years.

She let out a shaking breath, and he could feel the heat of it brush his mouth, so close was she. So close was his destruction.

He was iron. He was rock. He had been forced to become so. A man of no emotion. A man of nothing more than allegiance to an ideal. Knowing with absolute certainty that if he should ever turn away from that, he might become lost. That corruption might take hold of him in the way that it had done his father. Because he considered himself immune to nothing.

And so, he had made himself immune to everything.

Except for this. Except for her.

So small and fragile, delicate.

Powerful.

Not because of her success or her money. But because of the light contained in her beauty. A storm wrapped in soft, exquisite skin that he ached to put his hands on.

And when she stretched up on her toes and pressed her mouth to his, no finesse or skill present in the motion at all, he broke.

He wrapped his arms around her, cupping her head in one of his hands, shifting things, taking control. And he consumed her.

What she had intended to be a tasting, a test, he turned into a feast. If he was going to be destroyed, then he would bring the palace down with him. Then he would crack the very foundations of where they stood. Of all that he had built his life upon. Of all that he was. If he would be a ruined man, then the world would be ruined as a result. As would she.

He nipped her lower lip, slid his tongue against hers, kissed her deep and hard and long until she whimpered with it. Until she had arched against him, going soft and pliant. Until there was no question now who was in charge. Until there was no question now who was driving them to the brink of calamity. It was him.

He had made his choice. He had not fallen into temptation; he had wrapped his arms around it. He had not slid into sin; he had gathered it against his body and made it his air. His oxygen.

And she surrendered to it. Surrendered to him.

The white flag of her desire was present in the way her body molded against his, in the way that she opened for him, the small, sweet sounds of pleasure that she made as he allowed his hands to move, skimming over her curves, then going still, holding her against him so that she could feel the insistence of his desire pressing against her stomach.

He was a man of extremes.

And if she wanted a storm, he would give her a hurricane.

If he could not be a man of honor, then he would be a man of the basest betrayal.

It was the sight of that book sitting on the side table that brought him back to himself. Just a flash of normality. A familiarity. A reminder of who he was supposed to be, that caused him to release his hold on her and set her back on her feet.

She looked dazed. Her lips were swollen. Utterly wrecked.

Just like he was.

"Never," he said. "It will never happen between us."

"But… It already did."

He chuckled, dark and without humor just like the very center of his soul. "If you think that was an example of what could be between us, then you are much more inexperienced than I would have given you credit for."

"I…"

"The things I could do to you. The things I could do to us both. I could ruin you not just for other men, but for sleep. Wearing clothes. Walking down the street. Everything would remind you of me. The slide of fabric against your skin. The warmth of the sun on your body. All of it would make you think of my hands on you. My mouth. And you would try… You would try to use your own hand to bring yourself the kind of satisfaction that I could show you, but you would fail."

"And what about your brother? Would he fail?"

"It is why I won't do it. Because yes. After me. After this… Even he would fail to satisfy you."

And he turned and walked out of the room, leaving her behind. Leaving his broken honor behind, held in her delicate hands. And he knew it. He only hoped that she did not.

The sooner Matteo returned, the sooner Javier could leave this place. Could leave her. Matteo needed to do what he thought was best for the country.

But Javier would not stand by and see it done.

CHAPTER NINE

SHE HAD FAILED. It kept her awake that night. The sting of that failure. She was supposed to seduce him. It had been her one job. Granted, it had all gotten taken out of her hands, and she had a feeling that her own inexperience had been played against her.

Her heart hadn't stopped thundering like it might gallop out of her chest since.

She hadn't expected him to find her in the ballroom. That was the real reason she had been in there. Who hung out in an empty ballroom? But then he had appeared. And she had realized it was her chance.

She hadn't actually been sitting there scheming. She had been avoiding her scheme.

After her failure at the waterfall, and after...

The problem was, he had shared something of his past with her there, and she felt like she knew him better. Felt guilty for her seduction plan even though it felt like the perfect solution to her problem.

Because she knew on some level that if Javier were to sleep with her, Matteo would not want her anymore.

And she had been... She had been excited about it, perversely, because for the first time in her life she was attracted to a man, so why not take advantage of it? She didn't want to marry him. He was... He was an unyielding rock face, and she had no desire to be stuck with a man like that for any length of time.

But then she had been sitting there reading that fairy tale. And not only had she—through those stories—come into a greater understanding of his culture, there was something about the particular story of the beast she'd been reading that had made her understand him.

Transformed into something due to the sins of his father and so convinced that the transformation was a necessity.

That he had to sit in the sins, in the consequence, to avoid becoming a monster on the inside as well as a monster on the outside.

She had been so caught up in that line of thinking that when he had appeared, she had clumsily made an effort at seduction, and she had been carried away in it.

That was the problem with all of this.

She was a reasonable girl. A practical one. A businesswoman. Thoroughly modern and independent in so many ways, but she had been swept up in a fairy tale, and nothing that she knew, nothing that she had ever achieved, had prepared her for the effect that it was having on her.

For the effect that he was having on her.

She had been kissed before.

Every single time it had been easy to turn away. Every single time she had been relieved that it was over. When she could extricate herself from the man's hold and go on with her day, untouched below the neck and very happy about it thank you.

But she wanted Javier to touch her. And she feared very much that the vow he had made to her before he had stormed out of the ballroom was true.

That if it were to become more, she would never, ever be able to forget. That she would be ruined. That she would be altered for all time.

"That's ridiculous," she scolded herself. *It's the kind of ridiculous thing that men think about themselves, but it's never true. You know that. It can't be.*

The idea that she might fail in her objective to avoid marrying Matteo terrified her. But somehow, even more, the idea that she might leave here without… Without knowing what it was like to be with Javier was even more terrifying. And she despised herself for that. For that weakness. Because it was a weakness. It had to be.

Without thinking, she slipped out of bed. She knew where his room was. She had studied the plans to the palace, and she was familiar with it now. Had it committed to memory. She had a great memory; it was one of the things that made her good at business. And, it was going to help her out now.

With shaking hands, she opened up the door to her bedroom and slipped down the corridor. It wasn't close, his chamber.

But suddenly she realized. That wasn't where he would be. She didn't know how she knew it, she just knew.

Where would he be?

His gym. That made sense. She had found him there that day, and the way that he was committed to the physical activity he was doing was like a punishment, and she had a feeling he would be punishing himself after today.

No. She stopped.

He wouldn't be there.

The library.

He would be in the library. Somehow she

knew it. He would be looking at the same book that she had been earlier. She could feel it.

It defied reason that she could. And if she was wrong... If she was wrong, she would go straight back to her room. She would abandon this as folly. All of it.

She would leave it behind, and she would find another solution to her predicament. She would use her brain. Her business acumen.

Right. And you're still pretending that this is all about avoiding the marriage?

She pushed that to the side. And she went to the library.

She pushed the door open, and the first thing she saw was the fire in the hearth.

But she didn't see him.

Disappointment rose up to strangle her, warring with relief that filled her lungs.

But then she saw him, standing in the corner next to the bookshelf, a book held open in his palm. The orange glow of the flames illuminated him. The hollows of his face, his sharp cheekbones.

But his eyes remained black. Unreadable.

"What are you doing here?"

"I was looking for you," she said. "And somehow I knew I would find you here."

"How?"

"Because you wanted to read the story. You wanted to see how it ended."

"Happy endings are not real."

"They must be. People have them every day."

"Happy endings are not for beasts who spirit young maidens away to their castle. How about that?"

"I don't know. We all have that story. Every culture. Some version of it. We must want to believe it. That no matter how much of a beast you feel you might be, you can always find a happy ending."

"Simplistic."

"What's wrong with being simplistic? What is the benefit of cynicism? And anyway, what makes cynicism more complex?"

"It's not cynicism. It is a life lived seeing very difficult things. Seeing tragedy unfold all around you. Knowing there is no happy ending possible for some people. Understanding for the first time that when you have power, you must find ways to keep it from corrupting you or you will destroy the world around you. Great power gives life or takes it, it's not neutral."

"All right. But in here... In the library, it's just us, isn't it? What does anyone have to know outside this room? It doesn't have to touch anything. It never has to go beyond here."

That wasn't the point of what she was doing. She should want Matteo to know. She should want there to be consequences.

But she wasn't lying to Javier.

Because suddenly, she just wanted to take that heaviness from his shoulders. For just one moment. She wanted to soften those hard lines on his face. Wanted to ease the suffering she knew he carried around in his soul.

Because he truly thought that he was a monster.

And he believed that he had to be above reproach in order to keep that monster from gaining hold.

She had intended to taunt him. To ask why he was so loyal to a brother who left him behind to be a babysitter.

But she didn't want to. Not now.

She didn't want this moment to have anything to do with the world beyond the two of them.

Beyond these walls.

Beyond this ring of warmth provided by the fire.

The heat created by the desire between them.

She had never wanted a man before.

And whatever the circumstances behind her coming to be in this country, in this castle, she wanted this man.

She had waited for desire, and she had found it here.

But it was somehow more, something deeper than she had imagined attraction might be. But maybe that was just her ignorance. Maybe this was always what desire was supposed to be. Something that went beyond the mere physical need to be touched.

A bone-deep desire to be seen. To be touched deeper than hands ever could.

There was something inside of her that responded to that bleakness in him, and she didn't even know what it was.

Her life had been a whirlwind. Her loud, wonderful family, who she loved, including her father, even though he had wounded her as he had done. Parties. Vacations. Things.

The triumph in her business. The constant roar of social media.

But now all of it had faded away, and for the first time in her life…

For the first time in her life Violet King was truly self-made.

Was truly standing on her own feet.

Was making decisions for herself, and for no other reason at all.

This moment wasn't about proving herself to anyone.

It wasn't a reaction to anyone or anything but the need inside of her.

And she suddenly felt more powerful than she had ever felt before.

As a prisoner in a palace in a faraway land. Standing across from a man who should terrify her, but who filled her with desire instead.

And whatever this resulted in, it would be her choice. This, at least, was her choice.

She didn't have to close the distance between them. Not this time. He was the one who did it. He wrapped his arm around her waist and brought her against him.

She shivered with anticipation. Because the pleasure that she had found in his kiss surpassed anything else she had ever experienced, and just thinking about it opened up a wide cavern of longing inside of her.

When his mouth connected with hers, she whimpered. With relief. To be touched by him again, consumed by him again...

Only days ago she had never met him. She had been living a life she had worked for. A life that she loved. And she had been missing this one elemental thing without realizing it. Had been completely blind to what desire could feel like. To what it could mean.

And she would have said that obviously if she could wake up tomorrow and just be back at home, back in her bed, if she could never have found out that her father did such a thing to her, then she would have gone back.

Until now. Until this. Until him. And she didn't think it was simplistic. Because as she'd said to him, why was happiness simplistic? Why was desire treated like it was simplistic or base? Desire like this was not cheap, and she knew it. It was not something that came to just everyone, that could occur between any two people. It was a unique kind of magic and she reveled in it.

In him.

His mouth was firm and taut, his tongue certain as it slid between her lips, sliding against her own.

That sweet friction drove her crazy. Made her breasts feel heavy. Made her ache between her thighs. Desperate to be touched.

She felt slick and ready, for what she didn't quite know. Oh, she knew. In a physical sense. But what she was learning was that there was a spiritual component to this sort of attraction that could not be defined. Could not be easily explained in a textbook.

Something that went beyond human biology and went into the realm of human spirituality.

It wasn't basic. It wasn't base.

But it was elemental. Like something ancient and deep that had been dug up from the center of the earth. An old kind of magic, presented as a gift, one she had never even known she needed. But she did know now. Oh, she knew now.

His hands were sure and certain as they roamed over her curves. As if he knew exactly where she needed him most. He slipped his hands upward, cupping her breasts, teasing her nipples with his thumbs. And she gasped. He took advantage of the gasp, tasting her deeper, making it more intense. Impossibly so.

In fact, it was so intense now, she wasn't sure she would survive it. He was not a rock. He was a man. And suddenly, the differences between the two of them felt stark and clear.

And, like everything else that had passed between them, just a little bit magical. That he was strength and hardness and heat and muscle. And he made her feel like her softness might just be strength in and of itself. A match for his.

Her world was suddenly reduced to senses. The texture of his whiskers against her face, the firmness of his mouth. Those rough, calloused hands tugging at her shirt, at her pants. She pushed her hands beneath his shirt, gasped when her palms made contact with his hot, hard muscles.

She lived in Southern California. She saw a lot of beach bodies. She had already seen him shirtless in the gym, and she already knew that visually, he was the most stunning man she had ever beheld. But touching him... Well, maybe it had to do with that chemistry between them. That spiritual element. But there was something that transcended mere aesthetic beauty. It was as if he had been created for her. Carved from stone and had breath infused into him, as if he had been created for this moment, for her to admire.

For her to revel in.

She moved her fingertips over the hard ridges of his abs, and when he sucked in a breath, all those gorgeous muscles bunched and shifted beneath her touch, and the very act of being able to affect him like she did was an intoxicant that transcended anything made by men.

She moved her hands up over his shoulders, across his back. Admired the sheer breadth of him. The strength inherent there.

The whole world rested on his shoulders. So much.

And she kissed him. Not just with all the desire inside of her, but with the formless, indefinable feeling that was expanding in her chest. The deep resonant understanding that was echoing inside of her. Because of him.

Because she saw herself clearly for the first time because of this moment. And whatever happened afterward, that could never be taken from her. This could never be taken from her.

He crushed her body against his, her now bare breasts feeling tender against his chest. Her nipples scraping against his chest hair. And she loved it. The intensity of it. That was another thing. She hadn't realized it would be like this. In her mind, making love was something gauzy and sweet. But this felt raw. A feast for her every sense. The smell of his skin, the touch of his hands. The rough and the soft. Pain and pleasure. Desire that took root so deep it was uncomfortable.

A desperation for satisfaction and a need for the torment to be drawn out, so she could exist like this forever. Balancing on a wire, precarious and brave, suspended over a glittering and breathless night sky.

If she fell, she was sure she would fall forever.

But if she didn't fall…

Well, then she would never know.

Both were terrifying.

Both were exhilarating.

And when he laid her down on the plush carpet by the fire and pushed his hand beneath the waistband of her panties, she felt her control, along with that wire, begin to fray.

His fingers were deft, finding the center of her need, stoking the fire inside of her and raising the flame of her need to unbearable levels.

Dimly, she thought she should maybe be embarrassed about all of this. It was the first time a man had ever touched her like this. The first time a man had ever seen her naked. But she felt no shame. None at all. Because it was him. And that made no sense, because he was a virtual stranger.

But not in the ways that counted. Not in those places that no one else could see, or reach.

He was a beast, transformed by the sins of his father. And she was a captive because of the sins of hers.

They both had big houses. Wealth. Certain amounts of power.

They were both alone in many ways. But not here. Not now.

So there was nothing to be embarrassed about. Nothing to be ashamed of. When his mouth abandoned hers and began to move downward, her breath hitched, her body growing tense. He moved to her breast first, sucking one tightened bud between his lips, extracting a gasp from her, making her writhe with pleasure. He pressed his hand firmly between her breasts, his touch quieting her before he moved those knowing fingers back down between her legs. Teased her slick folds, pressed a finger inside of her.

She squirmed, trying to wiggle away from the invasion. Until he began to stroke the center of her need with his thumb, the strangeness of the penetration easing as desire began to build.

He kissed a path down her stomach, down farther still, and replaced his thumb with his wicked lips and tongue, stroking her inside in time with those movements.

She shivered, her desire building to unbearable levels.

"My name," he growled against her tender flesh. "Say my name. So that I know."

How could he doubt it? Of course it was only his name. She didn't care at all. Not for anyone else.

"Javier."

He searched upward, claiming her mouth with his, and she could taste her own desire on his lips. She wanted more. Wanted to taste him. Wanted to torment him the way that he had tormented her.

But he was easing himself between her thighs, the blunt head of him right there, causing a tremor of fear to rush through her. But that was stolen when he captured her lips again, kissed her to the point of mindlessness before easing deeper inside of her. Before thrusting all the way home.

The stretching, burning sensation took her breath away, but she didn't want it to stop. Because this was what she had been waiting for. This felt significant. It felt altering. This was the new, this was the different that she had known lay on the other side of this. The transformation.

And when he was fully seated inside of her, she lowered her head against his shoulder, shuddering against the pain, but embracing it all the same.

He froze for a moment, but then he began to move.

She was blinded by the intensity of it. That sense of him, so large and hard filling her like this. It made it so she couldn't breathe. Couldn't think. Couldn't speak. Couldn't do anything but surrender to this thing that was overtaking them like a storm.

She clung to his shoulders, clung to him to keep herself rooted to the earth. Rooted to the floor. To keep it so that it was still the two of them in this library. So that no other thoughts could invade. No other people. No other expectations.

It was just them.

She didn't have to be the best. She didn't have to be better than her brother. She didn't have to make herself important.

She simply had to be.

All feeling. No calculation. No striving. Just bright, brilliant pleasure, crackling through her like fireworks.

And she was back again, poised on that wire, with the endless sea of nothing and brilliance shining beneath her. She was afraid. Because she didn't know what might happen next. But he was holding her, moving inside of her, over her, in her. And all she could do was cling to him. All she could do was trust in him, in a way that she had never trusted in another person.

But that's what this was. That's what it really was.

The giving of trust, sharing it. Because as vulnerable as she was in this moment, he was too. Because as much as she had to trust him to hold her in his arms, she was holding him as well.

And even as she felt so feminine, vulnerable and small, she had also never felt quite so equal. Quite so happy in those differences.

But then, she couldn't hold on, not any longer. He thrust inside of her one last time, and she was cast into the deep. And what she found there was an endless world of pleasure that she hadn't known existed. So deep and real and intense.

He followed her there. His roar of pleasure reverberating inside of her.

And all the stars around her were made of brilliance and fire. And when she opened her eyes, she realized that the flames were right there. In the fireplace. And she was still in the library.

And Javier was still with her.

She could feel his heart beating just like hers. A little bit too fast. A little bit too hard.

She wanted to cling to him. But he was already moving away.

"This cannot be endured," he growled.

He pushed his fingers through his dark hair, curving his muscular shoulders forward. And even as she realized that the bliss, the connection they had just shared was over, she couldn't help but admire his golden physique, illuminated in the firelight.

"I didn't mind it," she said quietly.

"Why didn't you tell me?"

"Tell you what?"

"You were a virgin."

"Oh. That. Well, if it helps, I didn't really plan to be."

"You realize that makes this worse."

"How?"

"Because I have… I have spoiled you."

"I thought you said that was a promise," she said quietly. "A vow, if I didn't mistake you. That you would ruin me for other men."

"That is not what I mean now," he said, his tone feral. He stood up, and she went dry mouthed at the sight of his naked body.

"No. What do you mean? Perhaps I need clarification?"

"If you were a virgin, then it was meant for him."

"It was meant for who I gave it to."

"Did you give it to me? Or did you fling it away knowing what you were doing."

"No." She winced internally, not because she'd been thinking of her virginity, but she had considered the fact that this would make the marriage to Matteo difficult. But in the end, it wasn't why she had done it. "We don't all live in the Dark Ages, Javier, and you know that. I don't come from this world. Who I decide to sleep with is my choice and my business, and it is not a medieval bargaining tool, however my father treated me and my body. I do not owe you an explanation."

"But I owed my brother my loyalty."

"Then the failure is yours," she spat, feeling defensive and angry, all the beautiful feelings that she had felt only moments before melting away. "It was my first time, and you're ruining it. It was really quite nice before you started talking."

"But it is a reality we must deal with," he said. "You are to marry my brother."

"You can't possibly think that I will go through with it after this."

He stared at her, his eyes dark, bleak.

"You do. You honestly think that whatever this greater good is that your brother plans… You honestly think that it's more important than what I want. Than what passed between us here. You know that I don't want to marry him. Putting aside the fact that we just made love… You know that I want to go home."

Fury filled her. Impotent and fiery. She just wanted to rage. Wanted to turn things over. Because she felt utterly and completely altered, and he remained stone.

"How can nothing have changed for you?"

"Because the world around me did not change. My obligations did not change."

"This was a mistake," she said. "It was a huge mistake."

She began to collect her clothes, and she dressed as quickly as possible. Then she ran out of the library without looking back. Pain lashed at her chest. Her heart felt raw and bloodied.

How could he have devastated her like this? It had been her plan. Her seduction plan to try to gain a bid for freedom, and it had ended...

She felt heartbroken.

Because this thing between them had felt singular and new, and so had she. Because it had felt like maybe it was something worth fighting for.

But not for him.

When she closed the bedroom door behind her, for the first time she truly did feel like a prisoner.

But not a prisoner of this palace, a prisoner of the demons that lurked inside of Javier.

And she didn't know if there would be any escaping them.

When Matteo returned two days later, Javier had only one goal in mind.

He knew that what he was doing was an utter violation of his position. But he had already done that.

But things had become clearer and clearer to him over the past couple of days. And while he knew that his actions had been unforgivable, there was only one course of action to take.

"You need to set her free," he said when he walked into his brother's office.

"Would you excuse us, Livia?"

Like the mouse he often called her, Livia scurried from the room.

"You must be very happy with her performance on the business trip to address her by her first name."

"I am. Now, who exactly do I have to set free?"

"Violet King. You cannot hold her. You cannot possibly be enforcing her father's medieval bargaining."

"I instigated the medieval bargain. So obviously I'm interested in preserving it."

"She will be willing to offer her business services. But she does not wish to marry you."

"Why exactly do you care?" Matteo asked, his brother always too insightful.

"I slept with her," Javier said. "Obviously you can see why it would be problematic for her to remain here."

Matteo appraised him with eyes that were impossible to read. "You know I don't actually care if you've slept with her. As long as you don't sleep with her after I marry her."

"You aren't angry about it?" The idea of Matteo touching Violet filled him with fury. That his brother could feel nothing...

Well, he didn't know her. He didn't deserve her.

Matteo waved a hand. "I have no stronger feelings about her than I do for my assistant. She's a useful potential tool. Nothing more. What she does with her body is her business."

"I betrayed you," Javier said.

"How? She has made no vows to me. And I don't love her."

For the first time, Javier found his brother's complete lack of emotion infuriating. Because he had wasted time having far too many emotions about the entire thing, and apparently it didn't matter after all.

"Let her go."

"Now see, that does bother me, Javier. Because my word is law."

"And you wanted to know when you were overstepping. And it is now. She doesn't wish to marry you. She wishes to leave."

"And her wishes override mine?"

"You would force a woman down the aisle?"

"I told you what I wanted."

"And I'm here to tell you it isn't going to happen. She is mine."

"Then you marry her."

He jerked backward. "What?"

"You marry her."

"Why the hell does anyone have to marry her?"

"Because I made a bargain with her father. And I don't like to go back on a bargain. It was what he promised me in exchange for his freedom. I didn't ask, if you were wondering."

"He simply… Offered her?"

"Yes. I think he liked the idea of a connection with royalty."

"She doesn't want it."

"But you see, I made a business deal with Robert King. He gave me some very tactical business advice that was needed at the time. In exchange I promised that I would make his daughter royalty. Make him a real king, so to speak."

"In exchange for?"

"Manufacturing rights."

"Violet is prepared to offer those for her makeup line."

"Great. I'm glad to hear it. I would like both. Either I marry her or you do it, younger brother, but someone has to."

Javier stared at his brother, more a brick wall

than even Javier was. And for the first time he truly resented that his brother was the leader of the nation and he owed him loyalty. Because he would like to tell him exactly where he could shove his edict. Because they were two alpha males with an equal amount of physical strength and a definite lack of a desire to be ruled by anyone.

But his brother was the oldest. So he was the only one that actually got to give that free rein.

But Javier thought of Violet. Violet.

And he could send her away, or he could keep her.

The beast in the castle.

He could have her. Always. Could keep her for his own and not have to apologize for it.

"Why did you make it sound like her father didn't have any power? Like he'd lost a bet?"

"That's what he told me. He didn't want her to know that he had traded her for a business deal. He instructed me that when the time was right… I should embellish a little bit."

"That bastard."

"Honestly. He's decent enough compared to our father."

"Our father should not be a metric for good parenting in comparison to anyone."

"Perhaps not. So, what's it to be?"

"Even if I marry her, you will still have to marry."

"I'm aware," Matteo said. "I'm sure my mouse can help with that."

"I'm sure she shall be delighted to."

"She is ever delighted to serve my every whim. After all, I am her Savior, am I not?"

"I cannot imagine a worse possible man to serve as Savior. To owe you a debt must be a truly miserable thing. I will marry Violet."

"Interesting," Matteo said. "I did not expect you to accept."

"If you touch her," Javier said, "I will make good on my promise and find an excuse to kill you."

"So you have feelings for her?"

He had, for many years, looked into his soul and seen only darkness. But she had somehow traversed into that darkness and left the tiniest shard of hope in him. A small sliver of light. But it wasn't his. It was hers. He feared that the laughter she'd placed in him, the smile she'd put on his lips…he feared in the end his darkness would consume it.

But like any starving creature, hungry for warmth, he could not turn away either.

Though he knew he should.

Though it went against all he knew he should do, all he knew he should be. "She's mine. I'm not sure why it took this long for me to accept it. I'm the one who went and claimed her. You've kept your hands clean of it the entire time. If I'm going to go to all the trouble of kidnapping a woman, she ought to belong in my bed, don't you think?"

"As you wish."

"I do."

"Congratulations, then. On your upcoming marriage."

CHAPTER TEN

VIOLET'S ANXIETY WAS steadily mounting. Everything had come crashing down on her that moment in the library. The reality of it all. And then in the crushing silence Javier had delivered in the days since, it had all become more and more frightening.

She knew that Matteo was back.

But she still hadn't seen him. Everything was beginning to feel…

Well, it was all beginning to feel far too real.

When she had gone back to her room after they'd made love, her body had ached. Been sore and tender in places she had never been overly conscious of.

And her heart had burned. The sting of his rejection, of pain that she hadn't anticipated.

And she couldn't decide exactly what manner of pain it was.

That he had still been willing to give her to

his brother, that he didn't seem to care what she wanted.

That he didn't seem to want her in the way that she wanted him, because if he did then the idea of her being with another man would...

Well, it was unthinkable to her, and on some level she wished it were unthinkable to him.

That he didn't care that she wanted her freedom, because didn't the beast always let the beauty go?

But maybe this was the real lesson.

Because how many times had her female friends been distraught over one-night stands that had ended with silence? How often had they been certain that there was some sort of connection only to discover it was all inside of them? Violet had been certain that what was passing between herself and Javier had been magical. That it had been real, and that it had been real for both of them.

But that had been a virgin's folly. She was certain of that now.

And she was trapped here. Trapped.

For the first time, she knew that she needed to call home.

But not her father. Not her mother.

Instead, she took her phone out and dialed her sister, Minerva.

"Violet," Minerva said as soon as she answered. "Where are you?"

"Monte Blanco," she said, looking out her bedroom window at the mountains below.

Even the view had lost some of its magic. But then it was difficult to enjoy the view when you were finally coming to accept that you were in fact in prison.

"Why?"

It wasn't any surprise to her that her bookish younger sister had heard of the country.

"Well. It's a long story. But it involves Dad making a marriage bargain for me. With a king that I still haven't met."

"I'm sorry, what?"

"I'm serious. I got kidnapped by a prince."

"I... What is your life like?" she asked incredulously.

"Currently or in general?"

"I just don't know very many people who can say they've been kidnapped by a prince. At least not with such flat affect."

"Well, I have been. And it isn't a joke. Anyway. You lied and told the world that you had our brother's billionaire best friend's baby."

"Sure," Minerva said. "But Dante never kidnapped me."

"He did take you off to his private island."

"To protect me. That's different."

"Sure," Violet said. "Look. I don't know if I'm going to be able to get out of this. I'm trying… But I'm here now. I'm in the palace. Then… The worst part is… I… He's not the one that I want."

The door to her bedroom opened, and she turned around, the phone still clutched in her hand, and there Javier was, standing there looking like a forbidding Angel.

"I'm going to have to call you back."

"No. You can't say something cryptic like that and then go away."

"I have to. Sorry."

"Should I call the police?"

"I'm the captive of a king, Minerva. As in an actual king, not our last name. The police can't help me."

She hung the phone up then and stared at Javier. "Have you come to deliver me to my bridegroom?"

They hadn't been face-to-face since that night. The last time she'd seen him he had been naked. And so had she. Her skin burned with the memory.

"Who are you talking to?"

"My sister. Oddly, I have a lot on my mind."

"I spoke to Matteo."

She took a deep breath and braced herself. "And?"

"You are not marrying him."

A roar of relief filled her ears, and suddenly she felt like she might faint.

"You mean I'm free to go?"

"No," he said gravely.

"But you just said that I don't have to marry him."

"No. But you do have to marry me."

"I'm sorry, what?"

"It turns out that neither my brother nor your father were honest about the particulars of the situation. You may want to call him and speak to him. But my brother made a commandment. He said one of us had to marry you. But that sending you home was not an option."

"Except, what's to stop you from letting me go?"

"I refuse," Javier said. "He has turned your charge over to me completely. And that means you're staying here. With me."

"But I have a life, and you know that. We… We know each other."

"And you wanted me to be something other than what I am. You want to believe that I am a man made into a beast. But you never gave space to the idea that I might simply be a beast. Given free rein to keep you, I think that I will. We are very compatible, are we not?"

"You…"

And she realized that the strange, leaping, twisting in her heart was because she was as terrified about this new development as she was exhilarated.

This man, this beautiful man, was demanding she become his wife.

And he was the man that she wanted.

If his words had been filled with happiness. If there had been any indication that he felt emotion for her, then she would have been... She would have only been happy. But there wasn't. Not at all. He was hard and stoic as ever, presenting this as nothing more than another edict as impersonal as the one that came before it, as if they had not been skin to skin. As if he had not rearranged unseen places inside of her. As if he had not been the scene of her greatest act of liberation, and her greatest downfall.

"Just like that. You expect me to marry you."

"Yes," he said.

"I don't understand."

"There is nothing to understand. You will simply do as you're commanded. As you are in Monte Blanco now. And the law here is the law you are beholden to."

"But you don't care at all what I want."

"To be free. To go back to your life. To pretend as if none of this had ever happened. But it has. And you're mine now."

"Why? Why are you marrying me instead of him? I don't seem to matter to you. Not one bit."

That was when he closed the distance between them. He wrapped his arm around her waist and pulled her up against his body. "Because you are mine. No other man will ever touch you. I am the first. I will be the last."

She was angry then that she hadn't had the presence of mind to lie to him when they'd made love. Because it would have been much more satisfying in the end. To take that from him, when it clearly mattered.

"I will be the only one. Didn't I promise you? That no other man would ever satisfy you as I did?"

"Yes," she said, her throat dry.

"I know no man will ever have the chance to try."

"That's all you want. To own me?"

"It's all I can do."

There was a bleakness to that statement that touched something inside of her. This, for him, was as close to emotion as he could come. It was also bound up in his control. In that deep belief that he was a monster of some kind. He had told her he was not good, but that he had honor.

And she could see now that he was willing to leave her behind, embrace greed.

And on some level she had no one to blame but herself. Because hadn't she appealed to that part of him when she had seduced him in the library? Hadn't it been on the tip of her tongue to ask him why he was so content to let his brother have what he so clearly wanted?

But he didn't need her goading him to embrace those things now. He emanated with them. With raw, masculine intent. With a deep, dark claim that she could see he was intent to stamp upon her body.

Unknowing he had already put one on her soul.

It wasn't that he didn't feel it, she realized. It was that he didn't understand it.

Perhaps she had not felt the depth of those emotions alone. It was only that he did not know how to name them. Only that he did not understand them.

"And what will it mean for me? To be your wife?"

He stared at her, his dark eyes unreadable. "You did not ask me that. About my brother."

"Because I wasn't going to marry him."

She let the implied truth in those words sit

there between them. Expand. Let him bring his own meaning to them.

"There will be less responsibility as my wife. I do not have the public face that he does."

"And if I should wish to?"

"Whatever you wish," he said. "It can be accommodated."

"What about charities?"

"You know that we would actively seek to establish them. We must improve the view of our country with the rest of the world."

"My charity in particular," she said.

"Supported. However much you would like."

"The control of my money?"

He shrugged. "Remains with you."

"And if I refuse…"

"Everything you have will belong to my brother. And you will be bound to us either way."

"Then I suppose there is no choice."

There was. They both knew it. It was just a choice with a consequence she wasn't willing to take on.

And there was a still, small voice inside of her that asked if she still thought she was lost in the fairy tale.

If she was still convinced that she was the maiden sent to tame a beast.

Whatever the reason, she found herself nodding in agreement. Whatever the reason, she knew what her course would be.

"All right. I'll marry you. I will be a princess."

The announcement happened the very next day. Media splashed it all over the world. And she was compelled to put up a post with a photograph of the view outside of her bedchamber and an assortment of vague gushing comments.

"Will I be expected to give up all forms of social media?"

"No," Javier said. "Your visibility is appreciated. An asset."

"Indeed," she mused, looking at the glorious meal spread out before her.

"I will need a ring," she said. "It will have to be spectacular. Don't mistake me. It's not because I have any great need of a massive diamond. Simply that you want me to make some kind of a spectacle. Getting engaged to a prince will require that I have a very strong jewelry game."

"I will bring the Crown Jewels out of the vault for your examination, My Princess."

"Are you teasing me or not?"

"I am not."

The problem was, she couldn't really tell.

And the other problem was, in the days since the engagement announcement, there had been no further intimacy between them.

The sense that she had known him had dissipated with their thwarted afterglow, and now she simply felt... Numb.

"Well. I guess... I guess that would be acceptable."

It was more than acceptable to him, apparently, because as soon as they were finished with the meal, he ushered her into the library, which felt pointed, and told her that the jewels would appear.

And appear they did. Members of his staff came in with box after box and laid them all out on the various pieces of furniture throughout the room. On the settee, the different end tables, a coffee table.

She blushed furiously when her eyes fell on the place by the fire, where she had given herself to Javier and cemented her fate.

"This is maybe a little bit much..."

"You said you wanted spectacular. And so I have determined that I won't disappoint you." His dark eyes seemed to glow with black fire. She wondered how she had ever thought them cold. Now she felt the heat in them like a living flame inside her chest.

He moved to one of the end tables and

opened the first box. Inside was a ring, ornate, laden with jewels that glittered in the firelight. And she would never be able to see firelight without thinking of his skin. Without thinking of his strong body searching inside of her. It was impossible.

She blushed, focusing on the jewel. Then, those large, capable hands moved to the next box. He opened it, revealing a ring filled with emeralds. The next, champagne diamonds. Citrine, rubies, every gem in every cut and color was revealed.

"There are the rings," he said.

"I…"

"Would you like me to choose for you?"

At first, she bucked against the idea. But what did it matter? Their marriage wasn't going to be a real one anyway. So what did it matter what she wore.

The idea made her eyes feel dry, made her throat feel raw. Because something about this felt real to her. More real than the diamonds that were laid before her. More real than the stones around them. This entire palace was made of gems; why she should be surprised and awed at the splendor laid before her she didn't know. But they were not real. Not in the way that the conviction and need that burned in her heart was.

This man was.

A man. Not a mountain. Not a beast. No matter how much he might want to believe that he was either of the latter.

The ring didn't matter, on that level. But it would matter what he chose for her. In the same way that it mattered the first night they had been together that she had known that he would be in the library. Known that he would be holding that book. Known that whatever he said, he was seeking a connection between the two of them. To deepen it. Because it was real. It was there.

She had spent her life seeking connections. Using connections. She had spent her life trying to show her father that she was worthy. That she was just as good as her brother, Maximus. Just as charming and delightful as her sister, Minerva.

But with Javier it was just there.

Whether they wanted it to be or not. And she had to cling to the fact that something in that was real.

"You can choose," she said.

"Very well."

It was the ruby that he picked up between his thumb and forefinger. He didn't even have to pause to think. With his dark eyes glowing with a black flame, he took her hand in his and he slipped that ring onto her finger.

"Mine," he said.

"Mine," she returned, curling her fingers around his. "If I am yours, then you must be mine."

There was something stark and shocked on his face as she said those words. "I'm a modern woman," she returned. "I believe in equality. If you expect that you will own my body, then I will own yours."

He inclined his head slowly. "As you wish."

"I like it," she said, looking down at the gem.

"Good. Because there is more."

He went to the coffee table, where wider, flatter jewelry boxes were set. He opened first one, then another. Necklaces. Spectacular and glittering with an intensity that mocked the fire.

There was one made of rubies, one that matched the ring. He pulled it out, held it aloft. All of her words were stolen from her. Lost completely in the moment.

And for her, it wasn't about the value of the gems, but about the care of the selection. About the fact that he knew what he wanted to see her wear. That he had chosen them for her. The necklace settled heavily across her breastbone, and he clasped it gently behind her neck.

The metal was cold against her skin and felt erotic somehow. She shivered. Of course, agreeing to be his wife meant more of this. This touching. This need.

This need satisfied and sated when they needed it.

He looked up at her, slid his thumb along her lower lip. And she shivered.

"Last time I had you here you belonged to him."

She shook her head. "No. I never did."

The corner of his mouth curved upward, and she recognized it for what it was: triumph.

"The tradition of what royal marriage means has been lost in my family," he said, his voice rough. "Have you read any of the other books on these shelves?"

She nodded. "A few."

"Did you happen to read about marriage customs?"

"No."

"Then I will explain. Because service is to be given, first to the country. Those who are royal do not belong to themselves. They belong to Monte Blanco. The woman who marries into the family surrenders in the same way."

"What about a man who marries into the family?" she asked.

"Women cannot sit on the throne here."

"That seems…unfair."

"I have seen how heavy the weight of the position is for my brother. I would call it a blessing."

"But it's gender bias either way."

"You may lobby for a change when we are wed."

He didn't even sound all that irritated with her.

It made her want to smile.

"A marriage into the royal family is a surrender of self," he said. "Except…except between the husband and wife there is a bond considered sacred. Nearly supernatural."

He moved his hand behind her back, and on an indrawing of her breath he undid the zipper on her dress with one fluid motion. It fell down her body, pooling onto the floor. Leaving her in her shoes, her underwear, the necklace and that ring.

Her nipples went tight in the cold air, her lack of a bra not a consideration before this moment, but now, with his hungry eyes on her…

She shivered.

"They have surrendered themselves to the greater good. To the nation. But in the walls of their bedchamber they surrender to each other. They belong only to each other. And it is ownership, *querida*. Not a partnership the way you think of it in your modern world."

"But they own each other," she pressed.

He nodded slowly, then he moved to the couch, and picked up another box. He opened it up and revealed two thick, heavy-looking bracelets. Gold and ruby, matching the rest of the jewels.

He moved close to her body and she responded. Being bare as she was with him so near made it impossible for her to breathe. To think.

He took the first bracelet out and clasped it tightly on her wrist. Then he took the second and put it around the other.

She felt the weight of them, heavy in a way that went beyond the materials they were forged from.

He moved again. "Surely there isn't more," she said breathlessly.

"Surely there is," he murmured.

The next box contained cuffs that looked much like the ones on her wrists.

"Do you know what these are?"

"No," she said, the word a whisper.

"These are very ancient. They have been in my family for hundreds of years."

"Oh."

"Out of use for generations. They are deeply symbolic. And they are never worn in public."

"Where are they worn?"

He looked at her with meaning.

"Oh."

"They speak of this ownership that I feel. The ownership I told you about, in these royal marriages."

"Oh," she said again, her throat dry, her heart fluttering in her chest like a trapped bird.

"Permit me."

And she didn't even consider refusing.

He knelt before her. With great care, he removed her shoes and set them aside. Then he lifted his hands, hooked his fingers in the waistband of her underwear and drew them slowly down her legs. A pulse beat hard at the apex of her thighs, and she closed her eyes tight for a moment, trying to find her balance.

She was embarrassed, to be naked with him kneeling down before her like this. And she didn't want to look. But also… She couldn't bear to not watch what he might do next.

So she opened her eyes, looked at him, his dark head bent, his position one of seeming submission.

But she knew better.

He clasped the first cuff to her ankle. Then the second.

Then, nestled in those jewelry boxes she spotted something she hadn't seen before. Gold chains. Without taking his eyes from her, he clasped one end of the first chain to her ring on the left ankle cuff, then attached it to the one on the right.

After that, he rose up, taking the other gold chain in his hand, sliding it between his fingers and looking at her with intent. Then he repeated the same motion he had completed on her ankles with her wrists.

She blinked several times, trying to gather herself. She took a fortifying breath. "I don't understand," she whispered. "Surely these wouldn't actually keep anyone captive. They're far too fine."

"They're not intended to keep anyone captive. Not really. This captivity is a choice," he said, curling his forefinger around the chain that connected her hands. He tugged gently, and she responded to the pressure, taking two steps toward him. "It is a choice," he said again.

Understanding filled her.

Because he was giving her a moment now. To make the choice. Or to run.

It fully hit her now that it was a choice she had made. To stay here. To say yes to him.

She stood, and she didn't move.

She tilted her face upward, the motion her clear and obvious consent. He wrapped his hand more tightly around the chain, bringing her yet closer, and he claimed her mouth with his.

The gold was fine, delicate and such a soft metal. She could break free if she chose. But she didn't. Instead, she let him hold her as a captive, kissing her deep and hard. His one hand remained around the chain, and his other came up to cup her face, guiding her as he took the kiss deep, his tongue sliding against hers, slick and wonderful.

Hot.

Possessive.

He released his hold on her, taking a step back and beginning to unbutton his shirt, revealing hard-cut muscles that never failed to make her feel weak. To make her feel strong. Because wasn't the woman who enticed such a man to pleasure, to a betrayal of all that he was, even more powerful than he in many ways?

Maybe, maybe not. But she felt it.

This, this thing between them, was something that was hers and hers alone.

His.

Theirs.

Two people who belonged to a nation. But belonged to each other first.

She understood it.

He shrugged his shirt off his powerful shoulders and cast it onto the ground. Then, he wrapped his hand around the chain again and began to tug downward. "Kneel before royalty," he said, his voice rough.

And she did. Going down to her knees, the cuffs pressing against her ankles, the chain from her wrists pooling in her lap.

She looked up at him and watched, her mouth going dry as he undid his belt, slid it through the loops on his pants. She was captivated as the leather slid over his palm before he unclasped his pants, lowered the zipper.

And revealed himself, hot and hard and masculine. Hard for her.

A choice.

This was her choice. No matter the position of submission.

Just as when he had knelt before her, fastening the cuffs, it had appeared that he was the one submitting, but he had been in power. It was the same for her.

She reached up and circled her fingers around his length, stroked him up and down.

It was amazing to her that she had never been overcome by desire for a man in her life before, but everything about him filled her with need. He was beautiful. Every masculine inch of him. She stretched up, still on her knees, and took him into her mouth. He growled, the beast coming forward, and she reveled in that.

Because here was the power. Here was the mutual submission. That belonging that he had spoken of. She in chains, on her knees, but with the most vulnerable part of him to do with as she pleased. His pleasure at her command. His body at her mercy.

She was lost in this. In the magic created between the two of them. Even more powerful than it had been the first time.

Because she had all these physical markers of who she belonged to. And everything about his surrender proved that he belonged to her.

She kept on pleasuring him until he shook. Until his muscles, the very foundation of all that he was began to tremble. Until his hands went to her hair and tugged tightly, moving her away from his body.

"That is not how we will finish," he growled.

He lifted her up from the ground, setting her on the edge of the settee. Then he kissed her, claiming her mouth with ferocity. He moved his hand to her thigh and lifted it to his shoulders, looping the chain so that it was around the back of his neck. Then he did the same with the other, so that he was between her legs, secured there.

Holding her tightly, he lowered his head, placing his mouth between her legs and lapping at her with the flat of his tongue. Giving her everything she had given to him, and then some. He feasted on her until she was shivering. Until she was screaming with her desire for release. Begging.

Until she no longer felt strong, but she didn't need to. Because she felt safe. Because she felt like his, and that was every bit as good.

When she found her release, she was undone by it. The walls inside of her crumbling, every resistance destroyed. Defeated. And then, the blunt head of his arousal was pressing against the entrance to her body, and she received him willingly.

He thrust hard inside of her, her legs still draped over his shoulders, the angle making it impossibly deep. Taking her breath away.

Their coming together was a storm. And she didn't seek shelter from it. Instead, she flung her arms wide and let the rain pour down on her. Let it all overtake her. Consume her.

She held on to his shoulders, dug her fingernails into his skin as her pleasure built inside of her again. Impossibly so.

And when they broke, they broke together. But when they came back to earth, they were together as well.

And she realized that he was circled by the chains as well. As bound to her as she was to him.

And they lay there in the library, neither of them moving.

Neither of them seeking escape.

And whatever he had said about his brother mandating the marriage, whatever she had said about not being able to surrender to his country, she looked into his eyes then, and she saw it. Clearly for them both.

It was a choice.

She was choosing him. The same as he was choosing her.

And the only sharp part of the moment was wishing that he might have chosen her for the same reason that she was choosing him.

She had fallen in love.

As she looked into those fathomless black eyes, she knew that it was not the same for him.

CHAPTER ELEVEN

HE DIDN'T SHARE her bed that night.

It wounded her more than a little. She had hoped that…that she tested his control a little more than that. Especially considering he had reshaped her into a person she didn't recognize.

One who had agreed to stay here.

Who had agreed to marry a man she barely knew.

Except…

Didn't she know him? On a soul-deep level? It was terrifying how real it all felt. She loved him. He had taken such a large piece of who she was in such a small amount of time.

And with the same certainty that she loved him, she knew he didn't feel the same.

She wasn't even sure he could.

It didn't change her heart, though.

Maybe she could change his. She hoped.

First, though, she had to take care of her life.

She took a deep breath and fortified herself. Then looked down at her phone.

Violet knew that it was time to speak to her father. She had been avoiding it for weeks now.

And it wasn't that she hadn't received calls from her family in the time since her engagement to Javier had been announced. She had. The only calls she had been at home to were from her brother and from her sister.

Maximus had been stern, and she had waved off his concerns. Minerva had been... Well, Minerva. Thoughtful, practical and a bit overly romantic. But then, Violet herself was being a bit romantic.

And anyway, she had talked Minerva through her situation with Dante, when the two of them had been having issues, and so of course Minerva had been supportive of whatever Violet wanted.

But her parents... She had avoided them. Completely. Not today. Today she was ready to have the discussion.

Today she was ready to hear whatever the answers might be.

That was the real issue.

If she was going to ask her father for an explanation, she had to be prepared to hear the explanation.

But something had shifted in her last night. That decisiveness.

She was no longer hiding from the fact that she had chosen this. That Javier was her choice.

That being in Monte Blanco was her choice.

She took a fortifying breath, and she selected her father's number.

"Violet," he said, his tone rough.

"Hi," she said, not exactly sure what to feel. A sense of relief at hearing his voice, because she had missed him even while she had been angry at him.

At least, missed the way that she had felt about him before.

"Are you all right?"

"It's a little bit late for you to be concerned about that."

"Why? I didn't expect that you would be cut off from communication with me."

"I haven't been. I've been perfectly able to call and communicate with whoever I wished."

"You haven't come back to California. You haven't been at work. From what I've heard you've only given minimal instruction to your team. It's not like you."

"Well. You'll have to forgive me. I've never been kidnapped before. Neither have I been engaged to be married to two different men in the space of a few weeks. Strangers, at that."

"I meant to speak to you about this," he said.

"You meant to speak to me about it?"

"It was never intended to be a surprise. But I lost my nerve when it came to speaking to you after I struck the deal."

"I can't imagine why. Were you afraid that I would be angry that you sold me like I was a prized heifer?"

"I figured that if I could position it the right way, you would see why it was a good thing. Being a businesswoman is one thing, Violet, but a princess? A queen?"

"Well, I'm not going to be Queen now. I got knocked down to the spare, rather than the heir."

"What happened?"

Her father sounded genuinely distressed by that. "Do you really care?"

"It would've been better for you to marry Matteo. He is the King."

"No," she said, "it wouldn't be better for me to marry Matteo, because I don't have any feelings for him."

"Are you telling me you have feelings for… The other one?"

"Why do you care? You let him take me. You let me be kidnapped and held for reasons of marriage without explaining to me why. Without… Dad, I thought that I was worth more to you than just another card to be dealt from your businessman hand. You would never have done this to Maximus."

"Well, quite apart from the fact that neither of them would have wanted to marry Maximus..."

"Why not Minerva?"

"It was clear to me from the beginning that Minerva would not have made a good princess. But you..."

"I went on to build my own business. To build my own fortune. You didn't know that I would do that when you promised me to him at sixteen. And in the last decade you didn't have the courage to speak to me even one time about it."

"It won't impact your ability to run your business. I mean, certainly you'll have to farm out some of the day-to-day, but you're mostly a figurehead anyway."

"I'm not," she said. "I brainstorm most of the new products. I'm in charge of implementation. I'm not just a figurehead." Her stomach sank. "But that's what you think, isn't it? You think that I've only accomplished any of this because of my connection with you."

It hit her then that her father genuinely thought he had been giving her a gift on some level. That there was nothing of substance that she had accomplished on her own, and nothing that she could.

And he couldn't even see that. It didn't even feel like a lack of love to him. And maybe it wasn't.

It was a deeply rooted way that he seemed to see his girls versus the way he saw his son. Perhaps the way he saw women versus the way he saw men.

"It was a good thing that you did," she said, "when you took Dante in from the streets of Rome. You thought he was smart. You sent him to school. If he had been a woman, would you have just tried to make a marriage for him?"

"I know what you're thinking," her father said. "That I don't think you're smart. I do. I think you're brilliant, Violet. And I think you're wonderful with people. Women have a different sort of power in this world. I don't see the harm in acknowledging that. I don't see the harm in allowing you to use that in a way that is easier. You can try to compete with men in the business world, but you'll always be at a disadvantage."

"I want to be very clear," Violet said. "I am choosing this. Not for you. Your views are not only antiquated, they're morally wrong. That you see me as secondary to you, as incapable, is one of the most hurtful things I've ever had to face."

"I'm protecting you. No matter what happens with commerce, you'll always be a princess once you marry…"

"Javier. I want you to know that I'm choosing to marry him. Because I care about him. I'm not afraid of losing everything, Dad. Not the way that you are."

"That's because you don't know what it's like to have nothing," her father said. "I do. I didn't have anything when I started out. And I built my empire from nothing. You built yours off mine. Easy enough for you to say that you're not afraid to lose it."

"Maybe so," she said. "And I've always felt that, you know. That I built this off something that you started. And I suppose you could say that my marriage here is built off something that you started. But I'm the one that's choosing this. I'm the one that's choosing to make all that I can from it."

"Violet, I know that you're not happy with me about this, but clearly it worked out for the best."

She thought of last night. Of the passion that had erupted between her and Javier. Of the way that she felt for him.

It didn't feel like the best. It felt necessary.

It felt real and raw and closer to who she was than anything else ever had. But it wasn't easy. And it wouldn't be. Ever. Because Javier wasn't easy. And she wouldn't want him to be, not really.

She wished that he might love her.

The strength of their connection was so powerful she had to believe… He was wounded. She knew that. He was scarred by his past.

He would fight against his feelings.

But he had accepted the marriage. He wanted them to choose each other, own each other.

She was certain of nothing, but she trusted that commitment.

She had to hope that someday it could become more.

"It didn't work out for the best because of you," Violet said. "You can't take credit for what I felt. And believe me, the relationship I have with Javier I built."

She hung up the phone then.

She didn't know what she was going to do about her relationship with her father going forward. Though living half a world away was certainly helpful.

The kind of distance required for her to get her head on straight. That was for sure.

And now she had to clear her mind. Because tonight there was going to be a dinner with foreign dignitaries. And Javier had told her that in light of the fact he had no people skills, she was going to have to do the heavy lifting for him.

Conviction burned in her chest.

He needed her to be his other half.

And so she would be.

She would choose to be.

Perhaps if she went first, if she forged that path with love, he would be able to find his way into loving her back.

An impromptu dinner with foreign dignitaries was not Javier's idea of fun. But then, few things were his idea of fun. And if he had his way, he would simply walk out of the dining room and take Violet straight back to bed. But tonight was not about having his way. Unfortunately.

She looked radiant. She had sent one of the members of the palace staff to town and instructed them to return with a golden gown from a local shop. And they had delivered. She was wearing something filmy and gauzy that clung to her curves while still looking sedate.

Her hair was slick, captured in a low bun, and her makeup was similar to how it had been the first day they'd met. More elaborate than anything she had done during their time together here at the palace.

He found he liked something about that as well.

That this was her public face. And that the soft, scrubbed-fresh woman with edible pink lips and wild dark hair was his and his alone.

She was standing there, talking to a woman from Nigeria, both of their hand gestures becoming animated, and he could only guess about what.

But Violet was passionate about her charities. About businesses that centered around women, and he imagined it had something to do with that.

"She is quite something," his brother said, moving to stand beside him.

"Yes," Javier agreed. "She is."

Not for the first time he thought that she would be better suited to the position of Queen than being married to him.

"Come," Matteo said. "Let us speak for a moment."

"Are you going to have me arrested and executed?" Javier asked as they walked out of the dining room and onto the balcony that overlooked the back garden.

"No," Matteo said. "Had I done that, I would have made a much larger spectacle."

"Good to know."

"I wanted to thank you for following through with the marriage."

"You don't have to thank me."

"I can tell that you have feelings for her."

Javier gritted his teeth. "She's beautiful."

"Yes," Matteo agreed. "She is. But many women are beautiful."

Not like Violet. "Certainly."

"Without you, I never could have done this," Matteo said. "All the years of it. Making sure that the damage that our father was intent on inflicting on the country was not as severe as it might have been. You have been loyal to me. Even in this."

Loyalty? Was that what he called this? He had been a fox curled around a hen. Waiting, just waiting for her to be left alone. Vulnerable and beautiful and his to devour.

It had taken nothing for him to abandon his promise. His honor.

To prove that he was morally corrupt in his soul. Incapable of doing right if he led with his heart.

"You consider it loyalty?" Javier chuckled. "I slept with your fiancée."

"It does not matter which of us marries her. Only that it's done. I told you that. And I meant it."

"I didn't know it at the time."

"I brought you out here to say that you must not think our bond is damaged by this. And it must not become damaged by this. I don't want your woman."

"I didn't think you did."

"I would ensure that you do not labor under the impression that I might. Which I feel could drive a wedge between us. As I can see that you are… Distracted by her."

"Now we come down to the real truth of it," Javier said. "Do you have concerns about what you consider to be my state of distraction?"

"Not too many. But you must remember that we have a mission here. A goal."

"I am very conscious of it. In service of that goal, she might have been a better queen than anyone else you could choose."

"She will do well in her position as your wife. As for me… I will keep looking."

"You will never be him," Javier said, looking at his brother's profile. "Don't ever doubt that."

"I doubt it often," Matteo said. "But isn't that what we must do? Question ourselves at every turn. I often wonder how I can ever be truly confident in anything I believe in. Because once I believed in him wholeheartedly. Once I thought that he had the nation's best interests at heart. Once I thought our father was the hero. And it turned out that he was only the villain."

Matteo gave voice to every demon that had ever lurked inside of Javier. When you had believed so wrongly, how could you ever trust that what you believed now was correct?

"We have to remember. An allegiance to honor before all else. Because if you can memorize a code, then you can know with your head what is right. Hearts lie."

Javier nodded slowly. "Yes. You know I believe that as well as you do."

"Good."

He turned around and looked through the window, saw Violet now standing in the center of a group talking and laughing.

"It's made easier by the fact that I have no feelings." He shot his brother a forced grin.

"Good."

Matteo turned and walked back into the party, leaving Javier standing there looking inside. Whether he had meant to or not, his brother had reminded him of what truly mattered. Not the heat that existed between himself and Violet. But progressing their country. Righting the wrongs of their father.

Javier had his own debt to pay his country. He had, under the orders of his father, used the military against its people. Had arrested innocent men who had spent time in prison, away from their families.

Who he knew his father had tortured.

He had been a weapon in the hands of the wrong man, with the wrong view on the world.

He was dangerous, and he couldn't afford to forget it.

Nor could he afford to do any more than atone for all that he'd been.

Nothing, nothing at all, must distract him from that mission.

Not even his fiancée.

"Someone else can go with me."

Violet was becoming irritated by the stormy countenance of her fiancé. He was driving the car carrying them down to town, wearing a white shirt and dark pants, the sleeves pushed up past his forearms. His black hair was disheveled. Possibly because earlier today they had begun kissing in his office, and she had ended up on his lap, riding the ridge of his arousal, gasping with pleasure until she realized that she was going to be late for her appointment at the bridal store in town.

"No," he said.

"You're not allowed to see the wedding dress that I choose anyway."

"It doesn't matter. I will wait outside."

"You're ridiculous," she said. "If you're going to go wedding dress shopping with me, you have to at least look a little bit like you don't want to die."

A mischievous thought entered her brain, and she set her fingers on his thigh, then let them drift over to an even harder part of him. "Are you frustrated because we didn't get to finish?"

"Obviously I would rather continue with that."

His tone was so exasperated and dry that she couldn't help but laugh.

"If it doesn't impact your driving…" She brushed her fingertips over him.

"It does," he said.

She felt even more gratified by the admission that she affected him than she could have anticipated. She let that carry her the rest of the way down the mountain and into town. It was important to her that she get a dress from a local designer. It was part of an initiative that she was working on with King Matteo's assistant.

Livia was a lovely young woman, with large, serious eyes and a surprisingly dry sense of humor. She was extremely organized and efficient, and Violet could see that Matteo took her for granted in the extreme.

But between the two of them they had begun

to figure out ways to naturally raise the profile of the country, coinciding with her marriage to Javier.

Acquiring everything from Monte Blanco that they would need for the wedding was part of that.

When Violet and Javier pulled up to the shop, he parked and got out, leaning against the car.

She made her way toward the shop and looked back at him. He was a dashing figure. And she wanted to take his picture.

"I'm putting you on the internet."

His expression went hard, but he didn't say anything. And she snapped the shot, him with his arms crossed over his broad chest, a sharp contrast against the sleek black car and the quaint cobbled streets and stone buildings behind him.

And he was beautiful.

"Thank you." She smiled and then went into the shop.

Immediately she was swept into a current of movement. She was given champagne and several beautiful dresses. It would be difficult to choose. But the dress that she decided on was simple, with floating sheer cape sleeves and a skirt that floated around her legs as she walked.

She took a photo of a detail of the dress on a hanger and took all the information for the bridal store.

Because when all this was over, anyone with a big wedding coming up this year would want a gown from this shop, from this designer.

When she reappeared, Javier was still standing where she had left him. Looking like a particularly sexy statue.

"All right. Now you have to come with me for the rest of this."

They went through the rest of the city finding items for the wedding. They created a crowd wherever they went. People were in awe to see Javier walking around with the citizens like a regular person. Not that anything about him could be called regular.

"They love you," she said as they walked into a flower shop.

He looked improbable standing next to displays of baby's breath, hyacinth and other similarly soft and pastel-colored things.

"They shouldn't," he said.

"Why not?"

"Nobody should love a person in a position of power. They should demand respect of him."

"You have some very hard opinions," she said, reaching out and brushing her fingertips over the baby's breath.

"I have to have hard opinions."

He touched the edge of one of the hyacinth blossoms and she snapped a quick picture. She enjoyed the sight of his masculine hand against that femininity. It made her think of a hot evening spent with him. It made her think of sex. Of the way he touched her between her legs.

As if he were thinking the exact same thing, he looked at her, their eyes clashing. And she felt the impact of it low in her stomach.

"I'm definitely feeling a bit of frustration over having not gotten to finish what we started earlier," he murmured.

"Me too," she whispered. "But we are out doing our duty. And isn't that the entire point of this marriage?"

The question felt like it was balanced on the edge of a knife. And her right along with it.

"It is," he said, taking his hand away from the flower.

"Right. Well. I think I found the flowers that I want."

She spoke to the shop owner, placing her order. And then the two of them carried on.

"I think we ought to have ice cream for the wedding," she said, standing outside the store. She was searching for something. For that connection with him that they'd had earlier. That they'd had back when it was forbidden.

"I don't want any," he said.

"I... Well. I mean, we can order some for the wedding."

"I think you can handle that on your own," he said.

Her heart faltered for a beat. It felt too close to a metaphor for all that they were right now. She could also love him alone. She was doing it. But it hurt, and she didn't know if she was ever going to be able to close this gap between them.

"Of course," she responded. "I... I'll go and order it."

She did. Then she ordered an ice-cream cone for herself and ignored the pain in her chest. She ignored it all the way through the rest of the shopping, and when they arrived back at the palace and he did not continue where they had left off in his office.

And she tried not to wonder if she had chosen wrong.

She had to cling to the story.

Because eventually the beast would be transformed by love.

The problem was that her beast seemed particularly resistant to it.

And she wasn't entirely sure she understood why.

CHAPTER TWELVE

THE DAY OF the wedding dawned bright and clear. Violet was determined to be optimistic.

It has been a difficult few days. Javier's moods had been unpredictable. Some days he had been attentive, and others, she hadn't seen him at all.

He hadn't made love to her since the day he had given her the jewels.

They hadn't even come close since the day in his office, where they had been thwarted by her schedule. Something she bitterly resented now.

This distance made her feel brittle. Made her feelings hard and spiky, cutting her like glass each time her heart beat.

What would it mean to be with him like this, if it were this way forever?

When she'd imagined marriage to him, she'd imagined more nights like the ones they'd shared in bed together. With passion ruling, not duty.

But if their marriage would be like this…

She didn't know if she'd survive it.

She had bought a beautiful dress, a beautiful dress to be the most suitable bride she could be. What else could she do?

She knew that she couldn't wear the cuffs the way that she had done the day he had given them to her. But she did put two of them on one wrist and attached the gold chain, wrapping it artfully between the cuffs to make it look like an edgy piece of jewelry, rather than an intentional statement of bondage.

The day was made better and easier by the fact that her family was present. Minerva would be Violet's only bridesmaid.

Minerva looked radiant and beautiful in a green dress that skimmed over the baby bump she was currently sporting. She and Dante had taken to parenthood with zeal. They had been instant parents, given that it was a vulnerable baby that had brought the two of them together. They had adopted her shortly after they'd married, and then had their second child quickly after.

This third one had only waited a year.

"You look beautiful," Minerva said, smiling broadly.

"So do you," Violet said.

Falling in love with Dante looked good on

her younger sister. Violet would have never matched her sister with her brother's brooding friend. She would have thought that somebody with such an intense personality would crush her sister's more sunny nature. But that wasn't true at all. If anything, Minerva was even sunnier, and Dante had lost some of the darkness that had always hung over him.

He had maintained his intensity; that was for sure.

Of course, when he held their children protectively, when he looked at Minerva like he would kill an entire army to protect her, Violet could certainly see the appeal.

Really, what could she say? She had fallen in love with a beast of a man who was as unknowable as he was feral. She could no longer say that the appeal of an intense partner was lost on her.

"You really are happy to marry him?" Minerva asked gently.

"Yes. It's complicated, but I think you understand how that can be."

Minerva laughed. "Definitely."

"How did you manage it? Loving him, knowing he might never love you back?"

The corners of Minerva's mouth tipped down. "Well. Mostly I managed it by asking myself if I would be any happier without him.

The answer was no. I really wouldn't have been any happier without him. And the time I did spend without Dante was so… It was so difficult. I loved him so much, and I had to wait for him to realize that what he felt for me was love. He couldn't recognize it right away because… He didn't know what it felt like. More than that, he was terrified of it. And after everything he had been through, I could hardly blame him."

"Javier is like that," Violet said softly. "He's so fierce. A warrior at heart. And he believes that he isn't good. But that he has honor, and that's enough. He doesn't seem to realize that the reason honor matters to him is that he is good. And I think he's afraid to feel anything for me."

"Have you said that to him?"

Violet shook her head. "No. I don't want him to… I don't want him to reject me." It was one thing to be uncertain. In uncertainty, hope still blossomed inside her, fragile and small though it was.

But if she did say the words… If he rejected her definitively… Well, then she would not even have hope left.

"I understand that. But you know, it might be something he needs to hear. Because until he hears it, he's not going to know. Because he won't recognize it."

"I'm thankful for you," Violet said, wrapping her arm around her sister's shoulder. "I don't know very many other people who would understand this."

"My love was definitely a hard one," she said. "But I don't think it was wrong to fight for it. I feel like sometimes people think... If it doesn't just come together it isn't worth it. But the kind of love I have with Dante... There's nothing else like it. There's no one else for me. He was wounded. He needed time to heal. And it was worth it."

Minerva put her hand on her rounded stomach and smiled. "It was so worth it."

Violet smiled, determination filling her. This would be worth it too.

The love that she felt for him was so intense, it had to be.

It had to be enough.

Javier waited at the head of the aisle. The church was filled with people. Some who were from Violet's world, and many from his. Though he realized he didn't actually know any of the people in attendance.

He was disconnected from this. From the social part of his job. A figurehead.

It had been interesting going out into town with her. She drew people to them like a bright, warm flame drawing in moths. He had never experienced such a thing, because he was the sort of man who typically kept people at a distance simply by standing there.

But not Violet.

Everyone seemed to want to be around her. To be near her. He could understand why she had managed to build an empire over the internet. With people who wanted to look like her, be like her. People who wanted to experience a slice of what she was.

She was compelling.

And after today she would be his.

He gritted his teeth, curling his hands into fists and waiting.

She would come.

And the momentary hitch of doubt that he had was assuaged by the appearance of her sister, who walked down the aisle with a small bouquet of flowers.

He had met her sister for the first time this morning. The other woman had seemed cautious around him, and a bit wary. Her husband had been more menacing. As had her brother.

Her father had seemed shamefaced, and Javier felt that was deserved. Her mother had simply seemed excited to be in a palace.

Javier had no concept of a family like this. Large and together, even though they disagreed on things, and it was clear that they did.

Though, he imagined that most families that appeared dysfunctional disagreed on small things, and not whether it was appropriate that one of them sold another into marriage. But at this point, what was done was done.

And she would be here.

She wanted him.

And she seemed committed to serving her role for the country.

That was her primary motivation. She had made that clear in the flower shop.

And it was a good thing. Because he could not afford distractions. He could not afford to start thinking in terms of emotion.

The music changed and he turned his focus again to the doorway. Watching with great attention.

And then, there she was.

The sight of her stole his breath.

She was...

She looked like she did for him. Only for him. Her dark hair was long and loose, the veil that she had soft and flowing down her back. She looked almost as if she didn't have makeup on at all. Rather, she glowed. Her lips looked shiny and soft, her cheeks catching the light. It was magic. And so was she.

He had held himself back these weeks, because it had felt like something he should do until it was done. But now, here she was. Now she was his.

There would be no turning back.

When she reached the head of the aisle, she took his hand. And he pulled her to him. It was all he could do not to claim her mouth then and there. Not to make a spectacle of them both in front of the congregation.

And that was when he noticed the bracelets.

She had them both on one wrist. But the chain was there as well.

And when she looked into his eyes, he felt the impact of it all the way down to his gut.

She nodded slowly.

An affirmation.

She was choosing to give herself to him. And she was saying that she understood. The bond, the loyalty that traditionally existed here in this country between a royal husband and wife.

But he did not know where ownership fit into that. He did not know where duty and responsibility fit in.

He had told her about it. Mostly because he had wanted to see her wear those for him.

Those rubies and nothing more. But also he had... He hadn't understood. But suddenly, here, with those bracelets on her wrist, in a church, where they were about to make vows... Where she had brought the carnal into the sacred and blended them together, made them one, he could not understand how this bond could remain just another promise he decided to keep.

Because as she spoke her vows, low and grave in a voice that only he could hear, he felt them imprint beneath his skin. Down to his soul. And when he spoke his in return, they were like that gold chain on her wrist. But they wrapped around them both, binding them in a way that he had not anticipated.

He had thought he knew what this meant.

Because that day he had discovered the sorts of treachery his father protected. That day that he had realized that the orders he had taken for years had been in service of an insidious plan, and nothing that protected or bettered his people, he had sworn that he would uphold a set of principles. That he would not be led by his heart.

That he would not be led by anything other than a code of honor.

But now he had made vows to another person, and not an ideal.

When it came time to kiss her, it took all of his self-control not to claim her utterly and completely right there in front of the roomful of people. He touched her face, and he exercised restraint he did not feel, kissing her slowly but firmly, making sure that she knew it was a promise of more. A promise for later.

He had been restrained these past weeks.

But it was over now.

The vows were made. His course was set.

There was no turning back. Not now.

Whatever would become of this. Of them... It was too late.

You chose this.

He gritted his teeth against the truth of it.

It had been easy to say that he had done it for Matteo. That he was doing it to atone for the sin of taking her in the first place. But the fact of the matter was he was far too selfish to turn away from her.

The idea of giving her to another man had been anathema to him. An impossibility. Had his brother insisted on marrying her, he would have...

He would have betrayed him. He would have stolen her. Secreted her out of the country. Abandoned his post. Abandoned all that they had built.

The truth of that roared in his blood.

Like the beast that he was.

But there was nothing to be done about that now. She was his, so it didn't matter. She was his, so it couldn't matter.

He pushed it all away as he continued to kiss her, and when he was through, the congregation was clapping, and they were introduced.

But he didn't hear any of it.

There was nothing.

Nothing but the pounding of his blood in his veins, the demand that burned through his body like molten lava.

He would endure the reception for as long as he had to. For as long as he had to pretend to care about flowers and ice cream and all manner of things that were only stand-ins for what he had truly wanted all along.

He didn't care to touch the petals of an alarmingly soft purple flower. He wanted Violet. Her skin beneath his hands. He didn't wish to lick an ice-cream cone. He wished to lick her.

And he would play the game if he had to, but that was all it was to him. A game. A game until he could get to her. Because that was all that mattered.

She talked to her family, and he knew that he could not rush her away from them. She was speaking, even to her father, and though there was cautiousness between them, he wondered if she might make amends with him. Javier didn't know how.

He asked her that very question once they got back to their room. In spite of the fact that his blood roared with desire, he had to know.

"I don't know if it will ever be the same as it was," she said. "But it was never easy. It was never perfect. I can always see those sorts of tendencies in him. Those beliefs."

"But you will forgive him."

"Yes. I think sometimes... If you value your relationship with another person enough, you have to be willing to accept that they are flawed. I don't know that I'll ever be able to make my father see the world, or me, the way that I want him to. I can keep showing him, though. And in the meantime I can live my life. But cutting him out of it completely wouldn't fix the wound. It wouldn't heal anything."

"It might teach him a lesson," Javier said.

"I think having to watch me join with you might have begun to teach him a lesson," she said.

"What does that mean?" he growled.

"Only that you are a bit more feral and frightening than I think he imagined my royal husband might be."

"The beast, remember?"

"Yes. I think… We are husband and wife now. And I would like to know… Why?"

"Why what?"

"Why did you become the beast? The sins of your father. We talked about that. But it's deeper than that. I know it is. Because you changed when you found that little girl…"

"What do you think I was doing all those years before? I was seeing to his orders. Arresting men when he demanded that I arrest them. And women. Separating families as he commanded. And he would tell me it was for a reason. Because they were traitors. Because it was upholding the health of the country. But I realize now they were freedom fighters. People who wanted to escape his oppressive regime, and it was oppressive. That innocent people were put behind bars, tried and… I helped. I upheld his rule of law, and I regret it."

"You didn't know."

"Maybe not. But when you have believed so wholeheartedly in a lie, you can never trust yourself again. You can never trust in the clarity of your own judgment because you have been so fooled. Because you were a villain and all the while imagined yourself a hero. And you will never, ever be able to walk through life without wondering which side you're on again. You will never be able to take it for granted."

"It takes such courage to admit that. You are brave. And I can see that you'll never take the easy way. You can trust yourself."

He shook his head. "No. I can't. I love my father and I allowed those feelings to blind myself to his faults."

"Well. So did I with mine."

"Your father is not a maniacal dictator. As challenging as he might be."

"No. I suppose not." She put her hand on his face, and he closed his eyes, relishing the feel of her delicate fingers against him. "You saved that girl, Javier."

"But so many more I did not save. So many I harmed myself. Arrested. Sent to a prison run by my father, where they were undoubtedly tortured. There is no salvation for such sins. My hands will not wash clean. But I can use them to serve."

"I'm sorry, but I know you, Javier. You're not a monster."

"I must assume that I am," he said, moving away. "The better to protect the world from any harm that I might do."

"I don't think you are," she said.

"This is not a fairy tale. The things that I have done cannot be undone. I can only move

forward trying to do right now that I understand. Now that I have the power. It is not about
being transformed by magic. Such a thing is
not possible."

She moved to him and she bracketed his face
with her hands.

He had no chance to respond to that, because
she kissed his mouth, and he was dragged into
the swirling undertow of desire by the softness of her lips, the slow, sweet sweep of her
tongue against his. She was inexperienced,
his beautiful goddess, but she had a sort of
witchcraft about her that ensnared him and
entranced him.

That made him fall utterly and completely
under her spell.

How could the magic fail here? Because of
him. That had to be it.

She was made entirely of magic. Glorious
soft skin and otherworldly beauty wrapped
around galaxies of light. She was something
other than beauty. Something more.

Something that made his heart beat new and
made him want to defy a lifetime of commitment to honor.

He had devoted himself to believing only
in a code. A list of principles that helped him
determine what was right and wrong because
he knew full well that his own blood, his own

heart could lead him in the direction of that which would destroy him and all those around him.

His belief in that had been unwavering.

When he looked at her, his Violet, his wife, he knew that he could believe entirely in her. In her magic. In the way her soft mouth rained kisses down over his skin, in the way her delicate fingertips brushed over his body. The way that she undid the buttons on his shirt and tackled the buckle on his belt. Yes. He could believe in that.

He could drop to his knees and pledge his loyalty to her and her alone, seal his utter and total devotion by losing himself in her womanly flavor. By drowning in the desire that rose up between them like a wave, threatening to decimate everything that he had built.

And he didn't care.

Just like he hadn't cared that first time they had kissed in the ballroom those weeks ago, when she had belonged to another man and his loyalty should have stood the test of time but crumbled beneath all that she was.

She was magic. And she was deadly.

And now, just now, he did not have the strength to deny her. To deny them.

And so, why not surrender? Why not drown in it? She was his, after all. He had gone down this path weeks ago, and it was too late to turn back. He had made her his.

His.

And tonight he would make that matter. He would revel in it.

He stole the power of the kiss from her, taking control, growling as he wrapped his arms around her and walked her back against the wall, pinning her there, devouring her, claiming her as his own.

He had spoken vows, but they were not enough; he needed to seal them with his body. He needed her to know.

He needed her to understand.

The way that she destroyed him. The way that he was broken inside. So that she would know. And he didn't know why he needed her to know, just like he didn't know why he had been in the library that night they had first made love. Why he had been looking through that same book that she was, trying to read the same story and find some meaning in it.

To try to see through her eyes the way that she might see him.

And it shouldn't matter. It never should have. Because she had been his brother's and he had been toying with betrayal even then.

But she's yours now.

Yes, she was his. For better or worse.

He feared very much it might be worse. Because he hurt people. It felt like a natural part of what he was. That monster.

But perhaps if it was only this, if it was only lust, he could control it.

He wrenched that beautiful dress off her body. She was an Angel in it, far too pure for him, and it nearly hurt to look at her. Burned his hands to pull the filmy fabric away from her. But it left her standing there in white, angelic underthings. Garments that spoke of purity, and he knew that he was unequal to the task of touching them. Just as he had been unworthy of touching her in the first place.

But he had.

And he would.

He tore them away from her body, leaving her naked before him. Except for those jewels. The necklace glittering at the base of her throat, the cuffs heavy on her wrist, the chain wound around them. And the ring, his ring, glittering on her finger, telling the world that she belonged to him.

He had never had her in a bed.

He hadn't realized that until this moment. And tonight he would have her in his bed. Their bed.

She would not have her own room, not after this.

It was often customary for royal couples to keep their own spaces, but they would not.

She would be here. Under the covers, in his bed with him. Her naked body wrapped around his. Yes. That was what he required. It was what he would demand.

He picked her up and carried her there, set her down at the center of the mattress and looked at her. He leaned over, spreading her hair out around her like a dark halo, and then he stood, looking at the beautiful picture that she made. Her soft, bare skin pale against the deep crimson red of the quilt. She took a sharp breath, her breasts rising with the motion, her nipples beading.

"Such a lovely picture you make, My Princess."

"I didn't think my official title was Princess."

"It doesn't matter. You are *my* princess. *Mine*."

He bent down, cupping her breast with his hand, letting it fill his palm.

She was soft, so delicate and exquisite, and it amazed him that something half so fragile could put such a deep crack in the foundation of what he was. But she had.

He lowered his head and took one perfect, puckered nipple between his lips and sucked all her glory into his mouth. She arched beneath him, crying out in soft, sweet pleasure, and it spurred him on. He growled, lavishing her with attention, licking and sucking, stroking her between her thighs.

His wife. His beautiful, perfect wife, who threatened to destroy all that he was.

How had he ever thought that it was possible to maintain superior connections to this country. To duty and honor when the marriage bed presented shackles that could not be seen with the human eye. Perhaps that was why the cuffs existed. Not to create a sense that they were bound to each other, but to turn them physical. All the better to remove them when one chose to.

Because the ties that existed in his heart he could not see, he could not touch and he did not know how to unleash.

It was supernatural in a way that he would have said he did not believe in.

It was strong in a way he would have told anyone such a thing could not be.

And he was linked to her in a way he would have said he could not be to another human being.

Because he had given those things away so long ago. Because he had pledged loyalty to Matteo and not love. Because he had pledged his blood to Monte Blanco, but not love.

And what he wanted to give to Violet was

deeper, and he was afraid that she was right. That magic had always only ever been love, and that it could turn and twist into something dark and evil, just like magic.

All that magic that she was.

All that… He did not wish to give the word a place, not even in his mind.

And so he covered his thoughts with a blanket of pleasure, wrapping them both in the dark velvet of his desire, lapping his way down her body, her stomach, down to that sweet place between her legs. He buried himself there. Lost himself in giving her pleasure.

Got drunk on it.

Because there was nothing to do now but revel in it. Afterward… Afterward there would be time for reckonings and for fixing all of this. But not now.

Now was the time to embrace it.

The only time.

Here in the bedroom.

And maybe that was what the cuffs were for.

To create a space where the world didn't matter. Where there could be an escape.

And maybe for other men that would have worked. But not for him.

Because he didn't know how to create space.

He only knew how to be all or nothing.

How to be an agent of his father, or a war machine acting against him.

How to be a man, vulnerable and useless. Or how to be a beast.

But he had the freedom to be that beast with her. And somehow, with that freedom he became both. Wholly a man and wholly an animal in her arms, and she seemed to accept him no matter what. She shouldn't.

She should push him away. She always should have pushed him away.

But she had gone with him, from the beginning.

She had chosen to be with him.

And when he rose up and positioned himself between her thighs, when he thrust into her body, and when her beautiful eyes opened, connected with his, he felt a shudder of something crack through his entire body like a bolt of lightning.

She lifted her head, pressed her soft mouth to his, and he felt words vibrating against his lips. He couldn't understand them. Couldn't do anything but feel them, as the sweet, tight heat of her body closed around his.

She clung to his shoulders as he drove them both to the pinnacle of pleasure. And when she released, he went with her. Pleasure pounding through him like a relentless rain.

And then, he heard her speaking again, her lips moving against the side of his neck, and this time, the words crystallized in his mind.

The words that he had been trying, trying and failing, not to hear. Not to understand.

"I love you," she whispered. Her lips moved against his skin, tattooing the words there, making it impossible for him not to feel them. He was branded with them.

"I love you. I love you."

"No," he said, the denial bursting forth from him.

He moved away from her, pushing his hands through his hair. Panic clawed at him and he couldn't say why. He was not a man who panicked. Ever. He was not a man acquainted with fear. Because what did he care for his own life? The only thing he feared was the darkness in himself, and maybe that was the problem now. Maybe it called to the weakness that he had inside of his chest.

The desire to sink into her. To drop to his knees and pledge loyalty to her no matter what.

Even if she asked him to mobilize against his brother. Against his people.

And it didn't matter that she wouldn't.

What mattered was losing the anchor that kept him from harming those around him.

What mattered was losing the only moral compass he knew how to read.

What mattered was Monte Blanco and it was becoming impossible for him to hold on to that.

"I'm sorry," she said. "You don't get to tell me that I don't love you."

"I cannot," he said.

"Why not?"

"Haven't you been listening? Haven't you heard anything that I've told you? Love is the enemy. You're right. Magic. And magic can be dark as easily as it can work for good."

"So why can't you trust that between us it will be good?"

"Because I cannot trust myself," he said.

She put her hand on his chest and he wrapped his fingers around her wrist and ripped it away. She stared at him, the hurt in her eyes far too intense to bear.

Because he did not have the freedom to be himself with her. It was far too dangerous. And he had been lying. Evidence of his own weakness if it ever existed.

That he had wanted to pretend that what he knew to be true wasn't. That he wanted to give himself freedom when he knew that he could not afford it. This woman was a gift that some men could have. But not him.

Yet he had been weak, far too weak from the beginning to turn away from her. He'd been given every chance. Every roadblock in his personal arsenal had been set up. She had been intended for his brother, and if that could not keep him away from her, then nothing could.

She was dangerous. Deadly.

A threat to his own personal code in ways that he should have seen from the beginning.

Because she had been eroding the foundation that he had built from the beginning. Just a touch. A kiss. And then he had stormed into his brother's office to tell him that Matteo could not marry her. To tell him that he could not see through the plan that he had to make their country better, because Javier had wanted Violet for himself. He had never wanted to let her go. He would have gone after her. That much he knew.

But his brother had given him options that he had liked, and so he had taken them. Made it easy to keep on going down that slippery slope.

So he had done.

And now... Now he was sitting here in the consequences of it. She loved him. He could not give her that love in return.

He had broken not only his own sacred

vows, but in the end he would break her too. And that was unacceptable.

But he had married her. And that was done. Consummated. Presented before the entire world.

But they did not have to live together as man and wife. He could give her the freedom that she had wanted. But he could not give her this.

"Love is not to be," he said. "Not for me."

"I know that you don't trust it," she said. "And I understand why. But you have to understand that what I feel for you has nothing to do with the way you were manipulated into caring for your father."

"Was I manipulated? Or did I simply want to accept the easiest thing. The easiest reality."

"Do you think that I'm going to trick you into doing something wrong? Do you think that I'm secretly here to destroy your country?"

"No," he growled. "No," he said again. "It's not that. It has nothing to do with that. But a man cannot serve two masters. And my master must be my people. It must be my country. It must be to duty, and to honor. That is where I must pledge my allegiance, and I cannot be split between a wife and a nation."

"Then make me part of your people. Make

me one of those that you have a responsibility
to. Surely that can't be so difficult."

Except that he knew it would destroy her. It
was not what she wanted. It was not what she
deserved. And without it she truly would be
in captivity for all of his life. And he would
be her jailer. And so he was trapped. Between
violating all that he needed to be for his country and destroying the life of the woman who
had married him.

He reached over to her and unclasped the
first bracelet from her wrist. He unwound the
chain that she had wrapped there, and then un-
clipped the second bracelet.

Her eyes filled with tears as she stared at
him, but he knew that it would be a kindness.
It was a kindness whether she saw it that way
or not.

"What are you doing?"

"You are not my prisoner," he said. "And I
will not make you a prisoner."

"Now you say this? Now, after we've been
married? After I told you that I love you?
That's when you decide to give me freedom?"

"We must remain married," he said. "That
much is obvious. My brother would take a dim
view on there being a divorce so quickly. It
would cause scandal. And… I do not wish to
undo all that you have done for my country.

But you may go back to California. To your life. There is no reason that you must stay here. You do not need to be under my thumb."

"What if I choose to stay?"

"What you choose is up to you. But that will not alter my behavior. That will not change the fact that this place is my priority. That it is where my duty lies."

"I love you," she said.

She got out of bed, standing there, naked and radiant in the center of the room. "I love you, and you can't make it so that I don't. I love you," she said, like a spell, like an incantation, like she was trying to cast it over him, like she was trying to change the very fabric of what he was. Destroy him, then remake him using those words to stitch him back together.

As if she might be able to use them to take the beast and turn him back into a man.

"And I cannot love," he said. "It is that simple."

"You can," she said. "You can. But you're not a beast to protect the world from you, you have to be a beast to protect yourself from the world. You're afraid, Javier. You're afraid of being hurt again, and I understand that."

Her words lashed against something inside of him that felt tender and bruised. And he hadn't thought that he had the capacity to feel such a thing.

"You don't know what you speak of," he said. "You are protected. Even the betrayal that your father meted out to you was not one that might put you in peril or threaten your comfort in any way. He sold you to a king. That you might be exalted. You have no idea what I am fighting against. You have no idea what real suffering is. I have seen it. I have caused it. And I have to guard against ever causing it again. Do not give me your quick and easy sound bites, Violet King. I am not one of your internet followers. I am not impressed by quick, condensed versions of truth that are easy to digest. I have seen human suffering on a level that you cannot possibly understand. And I am related to the cause of it. If my life must be devoted to the undoing of it so that those in the future can simply live, then it must be. But don't you ever accuse me of being afraid."

And for the first time he saw her crumple. For the first time, he saw her bravery falter, and he hated himself for being the cause of that. He had plucked the woman from her office some weeks ago and taken her off to a land that she had never even heard of, and she had remained strong. She had remained stoic.

She had an answer back for everything he had said. But not now. He had finally taken that from her. He had finally destroyed some of what she was.

And there was no joy to be had in that.

It was confirmation. Of what he was.

That spark of light she had placed in him was now extinguished in her.

She had said he was not a monster, but he knew that he was.

That he would destroy her only more as the years wore on.

He hurt people.

He had caused pain under the rule of his father, and under the rule of his own heart, he would cause Violet pain as well.

"If you think that's what I meant, if you think that's who I am, then you haven't been paying attention at all. I thought that we knew each other. I thought that our souls recognized each other," she said, her voice breaking. "You saw me reading the book... And I knew that you would be reading it too. I knew it. You know the library was the first place that I looked for you that night we first made love. Because somehow I knew you would be looking at the same story I was, trying to see if you saw us in there."

"You misunderstand. I wasn't looking for

answers because I already have them. I understand that this was significant to you. That this was a first for you. But I have lived life. I have already had all the revelations I will have. Perhaps you can think of me as a lesson learned."

"What an expensive lesson," she said, her tone full of venom. "Wedding vows seem a little bit extreme."

"As I told you, the wedding vows can remain."

"Why would I stay married to you? If you don't want to have a real marriage?"

He gritted his teeth, fought against the terror that clouded his chest at the idea of losing her. He liked much more the idea of being able to keep her while keeping her separate.

"Do what you must."

He gathered his clothes and began to dress.

"Where are you going?"

"Out."

"I would never have thought that you would transform yourself into a basic sort of man. But that is very basic. Just out. No explanation."

"Because I don't owe you an explanation. Because you got the explanation that you were going to get already. That you thought there was more is your problem, not mine."

He gritted his teeth against the burning sensation in his chest and he walked out of the room, closing the door behind him.

Closing the door on them. On temptation.

Whatever she did now was her choice.

But he had done his duty, for honor.

Whatever she said, that was why.

He ignored the kick in his chest that told him otherwise.

He ignored everything.

Because that was the real gift of having transformed himself into a beast.

When he had done that, he had taken his feelings away as well.

So why did his chest hurt so much?

CHAPTER THIRTEEN

VIOLET WAS STUNNED. All she could do was sit there in the center of their marriage bed, alone. She had known that he would have an issue with her loving him. She had. But she hadn't known that he would do this.

Why now? Why had it come to this now?

All this time he could have set her free. He could have made this bargain with her.

And suddenly she felt very alone. Her whole family had been here for the wedding today, but she hadn't had enough time to speak to them. Would she have found strength from them?

She could call her sister. Her mother. Her father even.

She knew what Minerva would say, actually. Minerva would want her to do what made her happy. But Minerva would also say that sometimes difficult men needed you to believe in them until they could believe in themselves.

Because that was what had happened with Dante.

But no one had helped Violet up until this point. This had been the most independent she had ever been. Yes, it was somewhat enforced by the entire situation, but it was still true. She had to stand on her own two feet since she had been brought here. It had been difficult.

Difficult to face the fact that her relationship with her family hadn't been what she thought. Difficult to be thrown in the deep end of independence, when she had been so surrounded by the people that she'd loved for so long. The people that she had depended on for her entire life.

But all of this had been about choice. A lesson in it.

Ironic that she'd had to be kidnapped and dragged across the world to really face the fact that she wasn't her own person. Not that what she had built wasn't hers to some extent.

But she had been propped up for so long by her father, and then was angry about the fact that he had been controlling things from behind the scenes when she had...

She had been fine with it as long as it had benefited her.

Allowing him to invest money when she had needed it.

Knowing that he was there as a safety net.

But nobody was a safety net for her in this. Because her heart was involved, her emotions. And there was no one who could fix it but her.

Her and Javier.

But he had broken it, because he was afraid. Whatever he said, he was afraid.

She understood what he thought. Understood why he felt the need to protect himself so fiercely.

There might not be real curses in this life, but there was pain that could feel like a curse. Betrayal that could make you feel changed.

And there might not be magic spells or incantations, but there was something even more powerful.

Love was the magic.

And she was going to have to figure out how to make it work.

She didn't have a spell. Didn't have anything to make the fairy tale literal.

But then, the beast wasn't on the outside. It was inside of him.

And it wasn't made of the sins of his father, wasn't made of tainted blood. It was made of fear.

And love couldn't exist alongside fear. Because they would always fight with one another. Love demanded bravery, and fear demanded that you hide.

He was hiding.

He was the strongest, bravest man she had ever known, but in the face of love, he was hiding.

If she could understand that.

Because he had just taken her heart and flayed it open. And she had already known that love could hurt, because the betrayal of her father had wounded her so badly, and she had to make the decision to forgive him in spite of that.

Was that what she had to do here? Forgive and love until he could do the same?

She didn't know.

She found herself wandering to the library, because it was where she had found him before. It was where she had found some of the answers she had been looking for. Maybe... Maybe she would find them again here.

Because she wanted to understand. Because she had so many questions.

Why had he done this now? Why had he turned away from her now? Told her she could live a wholly separate life from him, go back to California...

He didn't do it until he was sure that you loved him.

That truth sat there, like a rock in her chest. He hadn't done it until he was certain of her love.

He had not done it until part of him was certain that she would stay.

And so that meant she had to, she supposed. Even if it was the hardest thing she had ever faced in her entire life.

The idea of staying with a man who didn't love her.

She went straight to the back shelf, but she couldn't find it. The book with their story.

The book was gone.

And that, above all else, gave her hope.

"What are you doing down here?"

Javier looked up from the book and at his brother.

"Where else would I be?" He asked the question somewhat dryly, and yet to him, it made perfect sense that he was here. To him, it made all the sense in the world.

"Not Dad's favorite dungeon," Matteo said. "But still, definitely a logical choice for somebody who is punishing themselves."

"Is she still here?"

"Who?"

"My wife."

"As far as I know."

"Are you certain?"

"Honestly, I didn't consider the whereabouts of your woman to be my responsibility.

I thought that was one of the perks of flopping her off on you. What has happened?"

"She's in love with me."

"Obviously," Matteo said.

"It's obvious to you?"

"Well. Not necessarily to me. But my mouse may have said something to the effect."

"Livia said something about it?"

"Only that she thought Violet seemed quite taken with you. And that it was probably a good thing she hadn't married me, all things considered."

"She's a fool."

"*Livia?* She's the least foolish woman I have ever known."

"No. Violet. She's a fool to love me. Anyone would be a fool to love either of us."

"It's true," Matteo said. "I don't disagree with you."

"So you understand that I told her I could not esteem her over the fate of the country."

"Is it a choice that must be made?"

"Yes. Because if the choice for Monte Blanco's well-being is not my ultimate motivation, then something else will replace it. And that makes me vulnerable."

"Vulnerable to what?"

He spread his arms wide. "To this," Javier said. "This. To being just like our father. A man with a favorite dungeon. A man who harms others."

"Is that what you think? That a mere distraction could turn you from the man that you are into the man that he was?"

"Haven't we always said that we must be careful to turn away from anything that might make us like him?"

"We must. I agree. But I suspect that you loving this woman will not bring it about. I think it is loving yourself above all else that opens you up to such concerns. Do you think that sounds right? Because our father never loved anybody. None of his corruption came from loving us so much. Or our mother, who we never even knew because she was dead before you ever took your first steps. No. Love did not cause what our father did."

"But I have to be vigilant…"

"Against what?"

"As we discussed, it would be far too easy to fall into another life. After all, wasn't it so easy to believe that our father was good because we thought we loved him?"

"What's the book?"

"Something that Violet was reading. A beauty and the beast story."

"What do you suppose you'll find in there?"

"An answer. Magic. I don't know. Some way

to change myself, because I don't know how else I might. To be a man for her rather than a beast."

"Maybe you don't need to change it all. Doesn't the Princess in the story love him without changing?"

"But she deserves better. She deserves more."

"What did she ask for?"

"Nothing," he said, his voice rough.

"Then why not offer nothing but yourself?"

"Because that is something our father would do."

"No, our father would take the choice away from her. Which is what… Well, that's what I did, in the beginning, isn't it? Our father would do whatever he wanted regardless of what she asked for. So why don't you go back to her? And find out what it is she truly wants. Listen. Don't simply follow your own heart. That's what men like our father did. Consider another person. See where it gets you."

"Maybe to disaster. Maybe to hell."

"How does it feel where you are now?"

"Like *hell*," he responded. "Like I'm a foolish man staring at a fairy tale asking it for answers."

"Sounds to me like you don't have any further to fall. And I need you to be functional. So sort yourself out."

"Are you advocating for love and happy endings now?"

Matteo laughed, shaking his head. "Hell no. The opiate of the masses in my opinion. But if you wish to join the masses, Javier, then I won't stop you. And if it is what Violet wants, then all the better that she didn't marry me. Because I would never be able to give it to her."

"Are you such a hypocrite that you would advocate for me what you don't believe you can have for yourself?"

"Not a hypocrite. Just a king. A word of advice. Javier, you were not born to be the King so don't take on the responsibilities that I carry. Take on your own. You're a warrior. And you were born to be. That is your position in this country. And the difference between you and our father was always compassion. It was the sight of that little girl being married off that changed you. That made you see. It was always compassion that made you better. It was always caring. Because a man who is in and of himself a weapon ought to have that sort of counterbalance, don't you think? In my estimation, love will make you stronger at what you do."

"And for kings?" Javier asked.

"A king should not be vulnerable." Matteo turned, then paused for a moment. "But it might be the only thing that keeps a beast from being dangerous. If you are so worried about hurting others, perhaps you should think about that."

And with that, his brother left Javier there, sitting in the bottom of the dungeon holding on to the book. And he knew that he would find no answers there. None at all. No. The only answers for who he was, who he might become, who he needed to become, lay with Violet.

If only he could find the strength in himself.

But perhaps, until then, he could borrow strength from Violet.

Suddenly the fairy tale made sense in a way that it had not before. His fingertips burned, and he opened up to a page with an illustration of the giant, hulking beast having his wounds tended by the delicate maiden.

Perhaps he was too focused on the transformation.

Perhaps he had not looked enough at what the story was really about.

As she said, almost every culture had a version of this tale. And in it, the beauty was seen by the reader to be the weak one. Put up against a dangerous beast.

But he was the one who changed. He was the one who transformed, because of the power of her love.

In the end, it was the beauty who held all the power.

In the end, it was her love that made the difference.

And so, he would have to trust in her power. Trust that, like in the story, she was more than able to stand up to the challenge of loving him.

He was the one who had to find his strength.

She had already proven that she had more than enough for the two of them.

CHAPTER FOURTEEN

SHE HADN'T GONE back to California.

Her social media efforts had begun to create more tourism in Monte Blanco, and she was working with the tourism bureau and local business owners on strengthening the market. She was still involved in her own company, with her VP holding down the fort on the local level back in San Diego.

She had begun spending more time in the city. She had rented office space and had begun working in earnest on her project to bring work to Monte Blanco. Specifically for women. She was in talks to figure out manufacturing, something that she was arranging with Livia, and she had already hired a few women that she had met at a local shelter to work on data entry.

She was having to do some training, and she had hired people to do that as well.

And all of it was helping distract from the pain in her chest, though it didn't make it go away.

She was still living in the palace. It was just that it was so big it was easy to not see Javier at all. And he had allowed that to be the case. He hadn't come to her.

She wouldn't go to him. But she was there.

Because part of her was convinced, absolutely, that she needed to stay. That he needed to know she was choosing not to run. That he needed to know that she was choosing this life. That it was not a kidnapping, not anymore. It was just a marriage.

And she wasn't the one not participating in it. That was him. He was the one who was going to have to figure out exactly what he wanted and exactly how to proceed. She couldn't do it for him. And that, she supposed, was the most difficult lesson of all. That no matter how much she wanted to, she couldn't force a transformation if he didn't want it.

He had to accept her love.

And right now he didn't seem to be able to do that.

She looked around the small office space, up in the top of the small, cobbled building. Above the ice-cream shop. It was so very different from all that modern glass she had left behind in San Diego. But she wasn't sure she even remembered that woman. The one who wanted things sleek and bright. The one who had been so confident and set in her achievements.

She still felt accomplished. It wasn't that she didn't know that she had done impressive and difficult things. It was only that she had found something she cared about even more. She had been so focused for so long. And it hadn't allowed for her to want much else. That had been a protection. She could see now. Because caring this much about something else, about someone else, was extremely painful. But it had also pushed her to find a strength inside of herself that she hadn't known was there. And so for that she was somewhat grateful.

Grateful, if heartbroken.

Because no man would ever be Javier.

She knew that she would never find another man she wanted in the same way. That she would never feel this way for another man. Because she hadn't. Not for twenty-six years. She had had chance after chance to find another man, and she had never even been tempted. And she wouldn't be. Not like this. Not again. But that didn't mean she couldn't thrive. It was just that she would never fall in love again.

Tears pricked her eyes. She didn't want to fall in love again anyway. She just wanted to love him. And she wanted him to love her back. Even facing the fact that it was impossible now didn't make it seem real. Because she hoped... She just hoped.

She wanted to believe in the fairy tale. But she was afraid that the real world loomed far too large. That the damage inflicted on him by his father would be the ultimate winner.

And she didn't want to believe in a world like that. But she had to face the fact that it might be all she got.

She went downstairs, stopping in the ice-cream parlor and getting herself an ice-cream cone, trying not to cry when the flavor reminded her of Javier. The owners of the shop hadn't asked her any questions about why they hadn't seen Javier. Why it seemed that she was always alone, the Prince nowhere to be found after the two of them had been so inseparable at first.

Plus, she had a feeling she just looked heartbroken. She was trying her best to get on with things, but it was not easy at all. She was strong. But strength didn't mean not shedding tears. Strength didn't mean you didn't mourn lost love. Or in her case... Love that could have been if it weren't for a maniacal dictator who had taken the love of a young boy and used it so badly. Made him think that he was the monster, rather than his father.

When she went back out onto the street, she stopped. Because there, down one of the roads, she saw a silhouette that looked familiar. And she flashed back to that moment she had been standing in her office. But she had imagined then that he was dangerous. And now... Now the sight of him made her heart leap into her throat.

"Livia told me I might find you here," he said.

"Livia is a turncoat," Violet said.

"She works for my brother. Her loyalty is always going to lie there."

"Well. *Well.*"

"I need to speak to you."

"Why?"

"I need to know... I looked for answers. I looked for answers that didn't have an enchantment or a spell. I don't know how to change."

"You don't know?"

"No," he said. His voice rough.

Her heart went tight, and she looked at his sculpted, haunted face. "Javier, it was never about the right spell. In all the stories, in all the lands, in all the world. It was never magic that changed the beast. It was love."

He shuddered beneath her touch. "I know.

But I looked and looked at that book. At this story." He held the book up. "The beast isn't the strong one. It's the beauty. It's her love. And still I'm not… I'm not fixed."

"Yes," she said, moving toward him, her heart pounding hard. "But don't you know what changes him? It's not just her loving him. It's him loving her back. Love is the magic, Javier. We might not have sorceresses and spells, but we have love. And that's… That's what makes people change."

Hope washed through her as she saw a change come over his face, his body. As he moved into action, swept her into his arms and pulled her up against his body. "Is that all I have to do? Just love you? Because I do. Because I have."

"Yes," she whispered.

"What if I hurt you? I am afraid… I have caused so much pain, Violet. All the years since don't make it go away."

"You have to forgive yourself. Because you're right, some things can't be undone. But people do change, Javier. You have. It doesn't wipe the past clean. But neither does a life of torturing yourself."

"If I hurt you… I am so afraid I will hurt you. More than I fear any other thing, more than I fear losing you, I fear hurting you. And that is what I could not accept."

"You won't," she said.

"You are so sure?"

"Yes," she said. "Because I saw the Prince beneath the beast the moment we first met. Even when I didn't know you, I trusted your word. You know the cost of selfishness, and you will never ask others to pay it. If you were your father, we would all know it by now. You simply have to believe it."

"What if I don't change?" he asked, the question sharp and rough. "What if love is not enough to change me?"

"I love you already. You're the only one who thinks you're a beast, Javier." She took a step back, putting her palm on his face. "*You* need to see the change. Not me."

"I love you," he said. "And I… You're right. I was afraid of what that might mean. Because I did love my father. Very much. But he was a monster. And I couldn't understand how I had been so blind to that. How I had seen only what I wanted to see. Because of how much I loved him. And I never wanted to be that way again. I never wanted to be vulnerable to making such mistakes. But I think… I think it is time for me to accept that I am a man, and no matter what, I will be vulnerable to mistakes.

But with you by my side… You have a compassionate heart, Violet. And perhaps the secret is loving other people. Valuing their opinions. Not shutting yourself up in an echo chamber of your own desires so that nobody ever reaches you. So that no one can hold you accountable for what you do. Our love will make me better. Loving you… Matteo said something to me today. He reminded me that our father never loved anyone. That it wasn't love that made our father behave the way he did. It was the love of himself. The love of power above people. I trust that we will find right. Good. That you will help me."

The plea was so raw. So real. Straight from his heart.

"Of course," she said, resting her head on his chest. "Of course I will do whatever you want. I will be whatever you need."

"But what do you get from this? What do you get from me? I need you. I need you to be a moral compass. I need you to love me. I need you to change me. What I do, I do for you."

"You showed me my strength. You gave me the fairy tale I didn't even know I was looking for. And I became the heroine of my story in a way that I didn't know I could be. You are my prince. And you always were. Even when you were a beast."

A smile tugged at the corners of her mouth, and she kissed him. Deep and long. And when they parted she looked into his eyes. "And if am being honest. I quite like you as a beast. With cuffs and chains and the lack of civility. Because you've always held me afterward. Because you've always treated me with care. Because you know when to be both. A man and a beast. And I think that's better than just having one. It makes you perfect."

"I thought... I thought that my father had doomed me."

"No. The sins of our fathers might have brought us together. But they don't define us. It's about us. And it's about what we choose. It always has been.

"That's the real magic. That no matter where you end up in life... You can always choose love."

"I choose love," he said. "I choose you."

"So do I." She bracketed his face with her hands. "But I must warn you. I have a debt to collect, Prince Javier."

"A debt?"

"Yes. You owe me for the rest of my life."

"What is it that I owe you?"

"Only all of you. And I intend to collect some every day forever."

"Then you're in luck. Because I intend to

give myself, all that I am, even the broken parts, forever."

"Excellent. I might still take you prisoner, though."

"I would happily be your prisoner."

"I shall have to figure out which of the dungeons is my favorite."

"Whichever one has a bed."

"Well. That I most definitely agree with. Did we break the curse?" she asked.

"I believe that we did."

"Magic," she whispered.

"Or just love."

EPILOGUE

"Princess Violet," came a rich, deep voice from behind her. "I believe I have a debt to collect."

A smile touched her lips, and she looked down into the crib at her sleeping baby, a girl they had named Jacinta, then back at her husband, who was prowling toward her, a wicked smile on his face. Man and beast become one.

That was how he loved her. And it was how she liked it.

Fierce and tender. Dangerous but utterly trustworthy.

"Do you?" she asked. "Because last I checked I was still the richest woman in the world, and a princess on top of it. I doubt I owe anyone a debt." She had continued to run her company successfully from Monte Blanco, and with the country having become the most photographed tourist destination in the world, a phenomenon and a craze in the last five years, her brand—now primarily manufactured there—had only become more in demand.

"This is not a debt that can be paid with money. Only with your body." A shiver ran down her spine. "And with your heart."

Javier was the best husband. The best father. He loved her even more now that they'd been married half a decade than he had in the beginning, and she never doubted it.

"I wanted a kiss earlier," he said, gruffly, nuzzling her ear. "You were too busy with Jacinta and Carlos."

"Carlos was eating paper," she said, in a voice of mock despair over their three-year-old son's taste.

"And I find I am still in need of my kiss."

So she kissed him.

"I find that is not enough," he said, and from behind his back he produced the jeweled cuffs. Anticipation fired in her blood.

"This is one debt I'm eager to pay," she said.

When she had paid—enthusiastically, and repeatedly—she lay sated against his body.

"You are right," he said finally. "You are magic. You have transformed me multiple times, you know."

"Have I?"

"Yes. From beast to man. Heartless to a man with more love than he can contain. You made me a husband. You made me a father. You made me love. You made me whole."

"Oh, Javier," she breathed. "This is the very best magic."

"Yes, My Princess," he agreed. "It is."

* * * * *

Wrapped up in the drama of Millie Adams's Stealing the Promised Princess?

You're sure to enjoy the first installment in her The Kings of California miniseries:

The Scandal Behind the Italian's Wedding

Available now!